"Let me help, darlin'."

Michael stroked her palms slowly with his thumbs as he spoke. "Is Clare in trouble? Where is she?"

Jennie almost told him. Her thoughts were clogged by the warm, sleepy male scent of him, and all she could remember was that once he had been her friend. Then, suddenly, another memory came to her. A memory of Quinn. And that was enough to stop the words from coming. She was ashamed of her gullibility. Michael wasn't there to help them—he was there to *expose* them.

"You'd like me to tell you everything, wouldn't you?" She laughed, a pleasureless sound that seemed hollow in the shadowy room. "Then you wouldn't have to do any work at all."

He smiled. "I won't have to do much anyway. It's a simple job."

She lifted her chin and looked into his deep brown eyes. He'd better learn not to underestimate her. "Good—maybe you can handle it then."

KATHLEEN O'BRIEN, who lives in Florida, started out as a newspaper feature writer, but after marriage and motherhood, she traded that in to write novels full-time. Kathleen likes strong heroes who overcome adversity, which is probably the result of her reading all those classic, tragic novels when she was younger. However, being a true romantic, she prefers *her* stories to end happily!

Books by Kathleen O'Brien

KATHLEEN O'BRIEN

Michael's Silence

Harlequin Books

TORONTO • NEW YORK • LONDON
AMSTERDAM • PARIS • SYDNEY • HAMBURG
STOCKHOLM • ATHENS • TOKYO • MILAN
MADRID • WARSAW • BUDAPEST • AUCKLAND

To Irene Farrell Pynn, with love and admiration

ISBN 0-373-11698-5

MICHAEL'S SILENCE

Copyright © 1994 by Kathleen O'Brien.

All rights reserved. Except for use in any review, the reproduction or utilization of this work in whole or in part in any form by any electronic, mechanical or other means, now known or hereafter invented, including xerography, photocopying and recording, or in any information storage or retrieval system, is forbidden without the written permission of the publisher, Harlequin Enterprises Limited, 225 Duncan Mill Road, Don Mills, Ontario, Canada M3B 3K9.

All characters in this book have no existence outside the imagination of the author and have no relation whatsoever to anyone bearing the same name or names. They are not even distantly inspired by any individual known or unknown to the author, and all incidents are pure invention.

This edition published by arrangement with Harlequin Enterprises B.V.

® and TM are trademarks of the publisher. Trademarks indicated with ® are registered in the United States Patent and Trademark Office, the Canadian Trade Marks Office and in other countries.

Printed in U.S.A.

CHAPTER ONE

JENNIFER KEARNEY had been hovering by the door, purse in one hand and car keys in the other, for twenty minutes. It was like being heart-deep in emotional quicksand. She stared out the window at the gloomy rain, knowing she must go. But her sister was crying, and the sound surrounded Jennie like a soft but inescapable prison, leaving her fingers incapable of turning the doorknob.

So she didn't move. She didn't speak, either—there was nothing left to say. She'd run out of good arguments fifteen minutes ago.

But how could she leave? Clare, her beautiful, indomitable older sister, was still crying. The wild tears had been spent hours ago, but silent new ones had risen to take their place, as if from a bottomless well of misery. Jennie's gaze fell on the slender body huddled in the window seat. With her voluminous white nightgown swamping her, Clare looked as helpless as a child.

Her own eyes stinging, Jennie glanced away, unable to bear the sight. Instead she searched the knotty pine walls for inspiration. There had to be *something* she could say to make Clare see how impossible her plan was. Clare couldn't hide in this island cottage forever. She needed to go home, if not to her husband, Alex, then at least back to the Triple K, the Kearney family ranch. It was the only sensible thing.

But Clare had never been sensible, and true to form, she wouldn't budge. According to Clare, the cottage was perfect. Perfect! As Jennie's gaze skimmed across the threadbare carpet and stained furniture, she sighed and felt the quicksand pull her down a little farther. Perfect?

Stewart's Roost, a small island just off the southeastern Texas coast, was never very popular with tourists. Even now, during the best summer months, it was practically deserted. Which was, naturally, why Clare had chosen it.

"I'll be back tomorrow," Jennie said finally, trying to break the spell that held her by the door.

"Don't come if anyone's following you," Clare said, jerking her head up. Her blond hair looked almost white in this murky light, and her face was pale. Jennie wondered if her own fair hair looked just as ghostly.

"Honestly, Clare." Jennie tried to smile. "Do you really think Dad would have his own daughter followed?"

"You bet I do." Clare's voice sounded as thin as crystal. "He's only been going easy on you because he's sure you'll tell him where I am eventually. You're his *good* daughter, after all."

Jennie felt herself flush. Clare made "good" seem like a synonym for weak—and she undoubtedly saw it that way. The good daughter. The daughter who smiled and obeyed and stayed out of trouble, while her defiant brother and sister raced about wildly, collecting exotic troubles like so many seashells.

Clare blew her nose angrily. "But once Dad realizes you're really not going to tell him, he'll go nuts. You know him. He's such a chauvinist—he'd never be on the woman's side of a problem, not even his own daughter's. To him I'm simply another uncooperative filly, and he's determined to lasso me and drag me back to the paddock." She groaned. "He'll never give up, just out of sheer cussedness."

Then let's go face him and get it over with, Jennie wanted to say, but she didn't. She'd suggested that—and a dozen other sensible ideas—over and over again in the two weeks that Clare had been hiding here. Clare refused them all, growing more frantic each day.

Though Jennie had offered to try to persuade their father to cooperate, Clare had been adamant. She didn't want Arthur Kearney brought into this situation. It was a private problem, Clare argued angrily, and if Jennie couldn't be trusted to keep it that way, then Clare would just run away from her, too.

Jennie had only to look at Clare's shadowed, haunted eyes to know her threat was real. Something was badly wrong between Clare and her husband, something Clare was not ready to talk about to anyone. If Jennie insisted on telling their father, she knew Clare wouldn't be in this little cottage by the time they came back for her.

But, whatever the problem, was hiding out really the only answer? Surely not. "Clare," Jennie began miserably. "Clare, I just don't see how—"

With a low murmur of desperate frustration, Clare turned her face away again. In the watery moonlight Jennie could see a tear slipping down Clare's cheek, and her throat tightened, shutting off the flow of timid words. Maybe she didn't see how yet, but somehow, *somehow,* she would protect her sister.

She had to. She was all Clare had. Their mother hadn't survived Jennie's birth, and their darling brother, Quinn, who had been so like Clare in spirit and daring, had been killed six years ago. Now it was Jennie and Clare against the world.

"Well, just in case Dad does hire someone, I'll be careful," Jennie said. "But I'll be back tomorrow. I promise."

She waited a second, but Clare, lost in her own black thoughts, didn't even look up. Finally Jennie opened the door, squinted into the cold, driving rain and made a run for her car.

An hour later it was nearly midnight, and she was still several miles from home, several million miles from an answer to Clare's dilemma and exhausted beyond anything she'd ever known.

Only the lure of her soft bed kept her going as she passed the acres of ranchland, all deeply asleep under the blanketing rain. She wanted to sleep, too. For about a week.

But no such luck. As soon as she turned into the long, circular Triple K drive, she spotted an unfamiliar car in front of the main house. It hugged the asphalt like a silent black shadow, the porch light picking out a gleaming curve here and a fragment of crystal headlight there. Its low-slung elegance whispered money, and Jennie muttered a curse at the sight of it.

Another of her father's business cronies! Her father, not content with dominating Kearneyco's corner of the computer software world, also fancied himself quite the gentleman rancher—though his foreman might disagree with the "gentleman" part of it. The two careers kept cattlemen, lawyers, bankers, breeders and accountants marching through the Triple K at all hours of the day and night.

Her father would, of course, expect her to act as hostess, tired or not. He would be furious if she refused to play her part. Well, too bad, she thought, nosing up behind the black coupe and killing her motor with a restrained violence. Not tonight.

The rain muffled her approach as she dashed up to the house. The door was unlocked, and in the entry hall two suitcases, as black and quietly expensive as the car outside, stood against the wall. Their presence confused her. Why suitcases? The business cronies were rarely invited to stay at the ranch.

She heard voices, and her eyes went immediately to the great room. All the lights were on, providing plenty of illumination for her to see quite clearly the man who stood next to her father. At the sight, her heart contracted painfully, and her purse fell to the tiled floor with a soft-leather sigh.

God help her, it wasn't another stout businessman in there, smoking her father's foul cigars and downing expensive whiskey. It was, in fact, almost the complete opposite.

The man who stared at her with unsmiling brown eyes was young—six years ago he had been only twenty-three. He was trim and muscular—those six years had added a couple of inches to his broad shoulders, making his hips seem trimmer than ever. And, six years ago, he hadn't been either a smoker or a drinker.

He had been something much worse.

His name was Michael Winters. And six years ago Michael Winters had killed her brother.

WHEN HE HEARD the front door opening, Michael had to force himself to stand up. Of all the faces in the world he didn't want to see again, of all the blue eyes he never wanted to meet, Jennifer Kearney's were at the top of the list.

Jennie's beautiful eyes. They had been full of tears when he'd seen her last, six long years ago. Her brother had died that night, died in Michael's arms, bleeding from a gunshot wound inflicted by what the inquest had eventually decided was "person or persons unknown." They had been hot tears of betrayed rage, because she blamed Michael and hated him for it. And then, when he had seen her at the hospital, he had reached out for her, to comfort and explain. But his hands had been covered with blood....

Oh, God, the look in those eyes then!

But now that he was here, in the same room with her, he realized he was going to see something in her eyes that he dreaded even more. More than hatred, more than sorrow. He was going to see Quinn. He balled his hands up at his thighs, as if to fight off the memory. Quinn.

Eight years ago, when Lieutenant Quinton Kearney had merrily invited Lieutenant Michael Winters home to the Triple K for Christmas leave, Michael had been amazed at how alike the three Kearney kids were. All with the same silky, golden hair. All with the same lively, dark-lashed blue eyes and the same graceful, tanned bodies born to do nothing more taxing than swim and play tennis and drive the opposite sex to distraction.

There had been a few subtle differences, which he had detected gradually during his frequent visits to the Kearney household. Clare, the oldest, was slightly harder, her gold dulled like a coin that had been handled too often. And Quinn had been restless, his blue eyes always looking for more excitement, as if life was his private Disneyland and he was already bored with the rides.

Jennie, the youngest—only fifteen when he met her, only seventeen when Quinn died—had been sweeter, and she had possessed a quiet core that somehow suggested an inner strength. Strength that was conspicuously absent in her brother and sister.

But that was ancient history. There was nothing sweet in the glare Jennie was directing at him now. With a merciless grip he shook himself out of the past and walked toward her. Though his voice seemed buried under a suffocating mound of emotion, he had to speak.

"Hello, Jennifer." Relaxing his fist, he put his hand out to shake hers. Cool and slim, her hand was as unyielding as a plaster mannequin's.

"It's good to see you," he said, hating the formal sound of it. That wasn't what he wanted to say. No, he wanted to say, *Did you ever forgive me, Jennie?* But he couldn't. Her cold hand—and eyes—wouldn't let him.

"Hello, Michael," she answered, withdrawing her icy fingers as soon as she possibly could. She moved away, putting her hands behind her against the rough-hewn fire-place.

An awkward silence followed, and Michael found himself staring at her, at how her golden hair, tied back in a glossy white bow, sparkled with silver raindrops. *Jennie*, he thought. *God, how you've grown up.*

Because she had. All the raw materials had been there six years ago—the eyes, the hair, the wonderfully sexy body. But back then she hadn't known quite what to do with herself, with her clothes or her makeup or her impossibly long legs. She had careened from one silly posture to another, from crimson-lipped vamp to tightly suited sophisticate. She had tried so hard to impress him, but—though she probably wouldn't have appreciated hearing it—he had always liked the natural Jennie best.

The real Jennie. Once, a couple of weeks before Quinn died, he and Quinn and Jennie had stayed up all night watching sappy Westerns. What a night! Jennie had been wearing nothing but one of Quinn's old football jerseys, cutoff blue jeans and a face full of creamy blue goop. The goop had dripped into the popcorn; she'd accidentally slathered scarlet toenail paint all over his knee; the dog had knocked over and licked up his beer. And it had been, for all that, one of the happiest nights of his life.

But that beguiling girl was gone now, replaced by this beautiful, incredibly cold young woman. And Quinn was gone, too.

She looked him over, raising one brow. "Well, well. Michael Winters. What brings *you* to Texas, I wonder?"

He frowned. Sarcasm sat like a foreign accent on her voice. Clare and Quinn had used sarcasm often and well, but he had never heard it before on Jennie's lips. Had she changed so much?

He'd often thought about coming back to Texas, about looking her up to see what changes the six years had wrought, but he'd never done it. Instead, coward that he was, he had barricaded himself in Seattle, doggedly building up his business, pretending the Kearneys no longer existed.

Now it was too late for pretense. Here he was, gazing into Jennie's eyes, watching suspicion and enmity slowly dawn in their blue depths. He found the sight surprisingly painful—surprising that is, considering how many cruel losses he had already survived. Best friend, wife, unborn child. After all that, what could the loss of this young woman's esteem possibly matter?

"Your father has asked me to help him with a few things," he answered, glad for every truth he could tell. His stomach clenched, anticipating the moment when lies would be necessary. He hadn't realized how much he would hate lying to Jennie.

As if sensing Michael's discomfort, Arthur Kearney activated his electric wheelchair, which whined as he rolled slowly toward them, crushing the huge roses woven into the carpet. At the noise, Jennie shot one hard glance toward her father, then returned her glare to Michael.

"I've asked Michael to look into some...problems," Arthur said with his usual brash authority, apparently ignoring the fury of her glance. "I've discovered I just can't trust some of my people," he continued, bringing his chair to a stop near his daughter. "So I've asked Michael to investigate things for me. He'll be staying here at the ranch. More convenient all around."

Even to Michael it sounded contrived, and clearly Jennie wasn't buying it. She never even looked at her father. Through the whole speech she stared at Michael, her mouth set in grim disgust. Michael felt her skepticism reach out like the scornful flick of a whip. She didn't believe a word.

Her full upper lip curled. And in the withering silence Michael understood that she knew. He couldn't think how, but she knew the real reason he had come. And she despised him for it.

He stiffened defensively. If he was going to make it through this assignment, he couldn't come unglued every time she tossed a disdainful look his way. This was his job, finding out things people wanted to hide, whether they liked it or not, whether *she* liked it or not.

It didn't matter. It couldn't be allowed to matter. Once they'd been friends and now they would not be, that was all. He would survive this, as he'd survived everything else in his life.

Finally she spoke. "Do you really think," she asked her father in clipped tones, "that *he's* the private detective you want? Staying here in our house?"

"You bet I do." To Michael's surprise, Arthur was smiling, apparently entertained by his daughter's barely contained anger. "He'll be with us twenty-four hours a day. Every day."

That was when Michael realized that Arthur *wanted* Jennie to know the truth. This was a battle of wills between father and daughter, and Michael had been brought in as the trump card.

"But to tell the truth I don't think he'll be staying long," Arthur added. "His private investigation company has dealt with some of the nastiest corporate hanky-panky in the country. I don't think he'll have much trouble getting to the bottom of our sordid little mess."

As Michael watched, Jennie reacted to the subtext of her father's words, her cheeks burning. Her pale skin had always been as easy to read as a thermometer.

"Oh, really?" She turned to Michael, her expression skeptical and goading. "You're that good?"

He shrugged in a fairly good imitation of indifference. He refused to flinch, though he knew where she was leading. Back to the night when, on his first job as a private detective, his carelessness had killed Quinn Kearney. "I'm not bad."

"Not bad? Then you must have improved a great deal."

Fighting to maintain his composure, Michael took a deep breath before answering. He'd known he would have to face this if he returned to Texas, and he had his answer ready.

"Yes, I have, Jennie. It's been six years," he said calmly, refusing to sound defensive. It was just a fact. Six years was long enough for a callow young man to mature, to master his profession, to learn from his mistakes. It was long enough for his world to shatter and be remade, misshapen perhaps, but more or less whole, from the pieces. Long enough to learn a little about love, and even more about loss.

She didn't deign to answer. With a scornful laugh she bent to kiss her father good-night, a perfunctory brushing of the air near his cheek that must have felt about as warm as a polar wind, and then began walking away from him.

"Six years, Jennie," Michael said again, more loudly, annoyed to hear that a defensive note tinged his voice after all. But she looked so damned judgmental. "It's been a long time."

She'd already reached the stairs, but she whipped around at that.

"Not to me," she said, and he saw tears in her blue eyes. The sight shocked him out of his careful cocoon. God, could it still be so close to the surface for her? Amazing. During the past six years, he had completely forgotten how to cry.

"To me," she said, her voice unsteady but distinct, "it seems as if it happened only yesterday."

"That's enough, miss!" Her father's voice was like a jerk on a bridle. He clearly expected his daughter to halt and behave. Michael had often watched Arthur use that very tone to reduce sweet Jennie to a subservient silence.

But much to Michael's surprise she didn't even blink. Oh, yes, Jennie had grown up. She merely narrowed her tear-filled eyes and lifted her chin. "And I can still see Quinn's blood on your hands."

Michael caught his breath, stunned by her cruelty, and instinctively he pressed his hands against his thighs, as if he, too, could feel the hot, red blood staining his fingers.

"Jennifer!" Arthur's hands were white as they gripped the arms of the wheelchair. "You will apologize."

"No," she answered him slowly as two tears rolled silently down her cheeks. "I don't think I will."

And then she turned and walked briskly up the stairs, not looking back even at her father's explosive noises of outrage.

"It's all right," Michael said in a stunned monotone so low it could barely be heard over Arthur's shouts. "It's all right."

But if Arthur heard Michael, he ignored him. Still barking furious commands, the older man propelled his wheelchair forward, obviously unable to accept that he had lost control of this, his youngest and most malleable child.

Alone in the great room, with the fire throwing shadows over the wood-paneled walls, Michael stood, letting the pain wash over him. Though his instinct, refined over a long, hard life, was to throw up a shield, to push the pain away, he forced himself to feel it, to endure every burning millisecond of it.

Perhaps, he told himself, sooner or later the pain he suffered would be enough to cancel out the pain he had caused.

And then he would be free.

CHAPTER TWO

ARTHUR HAD PUT MICHAEL in Quinn's old bedroom, just two doors down from Jennie, with only Clare's empty room between them, and in spite of her earlier weariness, she was wide awake when Michael's footsteps finally passed her door an hour after the rest of the house grew silent. He seemed to hesitate at the entrance to Quinn's room. She heard a small cough, or perhaps a deep sigh, and then the soft click of the closing door.

She wished she could believe the hesitation meant it was difficult for him, that he dreaded joining Quinn's ghost in that room. But the great Michael Winters didn't suffer from such sensibilities, did he? If he did, he wouldn't be here at all.

Sometime later she heard the whine of hot water through the pipes as he ran a shower. Against her will she lay in the darkness, listening, imagining him in there, draping his shirt across Quinn's chair, settling on Quinn's bed...

She froze, her fist bunched beneath her pillow, horrified at her thoughts. That tight feeling in her midsection was miserably familiar—even after six years she recognized it. She used to notice it when Michael put his arm around her, however playfully, or winked at her from across the room.

The feeling had been confusing at first. It was a bit like the delicious fear that gripped her at a scary movie—a slight, stumbling hiccup of her heartbeat, and below that a burning tightness that somehow felt heavy.

A strange reaction, but addictive. Experimenting with it, she'd soon learned that she could intensify the feeling to the point of breathlessness just by imagining Michael kissing her. Beyond that the details were hazy, but the sensations grew so intense she felt shaky, damp with tension.

After Quinn died, though, the fantasies had disappeared, and she'd believed they were gone forever. She couldn't think of Michael's hands without seeing blood on them, and the thought of him touching her skin made her feel physically ill.

She sat up in bed, her knees against her chest, and wrapped her arms tightly around her shins as if she could squeeze the sensual reactions out of her traitorous body. How could she be feeling this way about the man who was responsible for Quinn's death? Was it possible that desire could outlive grief?

She leaned her head against the headboard. Well, whatever it was, she wouldn't allow it. She wasn't seventeen and constantly at the mercy of her hormones. She didn't have to glow just because Michael was nearby, like the automatic floodlights above the patio that were set to blink on at the slightest vibration.

She shoved her pillow with a sharp punch. She would concentrate on reviving her anger. She'd neglected it in recent years, and it had weakened from disuse.

But it was still there. She felt its heat as she consciously fanned the flames. How dare he come back here? He knew he wasn't welcome. The last time she'd seen him she had given her fury free rein, making it clear she blamed him for Quinn's death. She'd never forget the names she had called him. It was almost as if she'd been trying to provoke a response from him, trying to force him to defend himself. But he hadn't even tried. He hadn't offered a single excuse for what had happened, instead letting her accusations beat against his silence like a wild storm against an unyielding rock. Somehow that silence was the most damning evidence of all. He had said nothing, she knew, because there was nothing to say.

Suddenly she was on fire with resentment. She wouldn't tolerate him coming back into their lives, living in her house, in Quinn's room. She wouldn't allow him to meddle in Clare's marriage, no matter what her father said.

Throwing the covers aside, she stood up, grabbed her robe from the foot of the bed, marched down the dimly lit hall and rapped hard on Quinn's door.

It took Michael a long minute to answer, and she had a brief flash of discomfort wondering whether he had even been dressed. Did he sleep in pajamas, or— Her fist fell slowly to her side as doubts set in, but she held her ground.

Finally the door swung open and Michael stood there, tying the knot of his pajama trousers and looking sleepily concerned. The bedroom was pitch dark behind him.

"Jennie?" He frowned, taking in her disheveled state. She realized belatedly that her hair must be a mess from all that tossing and turning. "What is it? Are you all right?"

"No," she said flatly, struggling to work herself up to her earlier pitch of righteous indignation. "I'm not."

He put his hand out and touched her upper arm gently. "What's wrong, darlin'?"

His voice was thick—he must have been sound asleep— and it was filled with that sexy Texas drawl that had always seemed to vibrate against some hidden place inside her. She shivered, goose bumps rising under his fingers. How many times had he touched her with this same casual affection? How many times had he called her "darlin'" in just that slow and tender way? Texas boys did that, and it didn't mean a thing.

But her body wasn't listening. It was seventeen again, and so heavy with longing that she felt hopelessly vulnerable, like a sun-flushed pear that would fall into his hands at the slightest touch. "Easy pickings," she'd often heard Quinn say, scornfully assessing some infatuated girl. Now she knew what he meant.

Damn! She pulled away from his fingers, disgusted with herself.

"What's wrong, Michael," she said tightly, "is you." She swallowed. "Your being here is wrong."

His gaze was clearing now, and he seemed more fully awake. He raised his right arm above his head, resting it against the edge of the open door. In that position the hall light fell on the dark, silky hollow under his arm and then drifted with a honeyed glow down one side of his torso, highlighting the dusky circle of his nipple and the ridged strength of his ribs. She moved back another step instinctively.

"Really?" A half smile curved his wide mouth, and putting his left hand on his hip, he leaned his forehead against his upraised forearm. "Why's that?"

"You know why," she said, and the force required to push the words out made them sound unnaturally loud in the silent hall. "You have no business being here. You're not welcome."

"Yes, I am," he said pleasantly. "Your father invited me."

"Well, I didn't!" Her voice was shrill and unpleasant—she could hear it, but she couldn't seem to stop herself. "I want you to leave," she said desperately, wishing she could slap that smug smile off his face. "I want you to get out of here!"

"Shh!" Grabbing her hand, this time without any gentle concern whatsoever, he yanked her into the shadowy room and shoved the door shut behind her. "Damn it, Jennie! Do you want to wake the whole house?"

She blinked, trying to accustom herself to the darkness, but she couldn't see anything except the dense mass of his body in front of hers. It gave her a peculiarly claustrophobic feeling, and she struggled, trying to free herself from his hold.

"I won't wake anyone. My father and his nurse sleep downstairs. You know that." She felt blindly behind her for the doorknob, but encountered his fingers instead, which clamped around hers with a firm grip that allowed no further struggles.

"You'll wake people over on the next spread if you don't get hold of yourself," he muttered. He exerted a slight downward pressure on both of her arms, which, though entirely painless, demonstrated clearly that he was in control. "Now settle down, Jennie, and talk to me."

"I don't want to talk to you." Like a fool, she continued to try to free herself, but with her arms incapacitated she could only wriggle from the torso and hips, and she ended up rubbing herself against the length of him in a way that was wildly unsettling. "I want you to leave."

"Why?" He pressed forward, just a fraction of an inch, but enough to bring her back in contact with the door, letting her see that escape was impossible. It also brought her in contact with every inch of his body, which the loose cotton pajamas didn't really conceal. She went completely still and tried not to feel the warm strength of his thighs against hers.

"Don't play dumb, Michael," she said, her voice low and tense. "We both know why you're here. But don't you see? You're meddling in something that isn't any of your business. You don't know anything about this."

She thought of Clare, alone on that damp, overgrown island, and her voice broke slightly. "You just don't understand, Michael. You don't know what's going on here."

She ended with a low sob, and at the sound his grip loosened. He murmured her name, and his fingers released her wrists and slid around to twine with hers. Up and down the length of him, his body softened against her. When he finally spoke, his voice had softened, too.

"No, Jennie, I don't know," he said gently. "Maybe you should tell me."

For a minute she couldn't answer, her defenses breached by the sudden about-face. With just a few subtle adjustments, he had shifted from captor to comforter, turning his offensive restraint into something that felt more like an embrace. She was confused, her thoughts clogged by the warm, sleepy male scent of him in her nostrils.

When she didn't speak, he stroked her palms slowly with his thumbs. "Come on, Jennie, darlin'," he whispered. "Let me help. Is Clare in trouble? Where is she?"

She almost told him. He had been her friend once, and he'd been such a good one. She remembered the night he'd found her by the stables, crying because no one had asked her to a dance. She'd been fifteen, with no shape at all, convinced she would be an ugly duckling till she died.

But he had dried her tears. He could already see how beautiful she would be, he said, how boys would be fighting for the chance to take her places. And then he had kissed her, his lips soft and sweet and light, because he wanted to be the first—the first, he promised, of many.

She fell a little in love with him that night, with his kindness, and his kiss, and with how strong and safe his chest felt under her cheek as she cried into his Army uniform.

The chest would be even stronger now, she could tell. He'd always been fit, but now his chest had the firm, glossy, rounded musculature of a hard-driven body. His work sometimes posed dangers, and he obviously kept himself ready to meet them. He mustn't be caught as Quinn had, too young, too naive, too pampered by an indulgent life to defend himself.

Quinn. That memory alone was enough to stop the words from coming, and her parted lips pressed shut. Tell him where Clare was? Why? Hadn't Michael already proved how unreliable his promises were? She'd already lost one sibling to his incompetence. Did she really believe he had changed—that he would use those rock-hard muscles to help Clare?

She recoiled, ashamed of her gullibility. He wasn't here to *protect* Clare or herself—far from it. He was here to expose them.

"You'd like that, wouldn't you?" She took advantage of his relaxed hold to slip out from her prison between his body and the door. Once clear of him, she tried to remember exactly where the furniture was. It was harder than it should have been—her body was clear of his hold, but her brain wasn't yet. Not quite.

A chair just to the left of the door, then the small table, then the dresser. Her mind snagged on the memories. Memories of Quinn standing at that dresser, tossing things impatiently as he searched for the perfect cuff links....

Beyond the dresser was the door to the bathroom, which thankfully had a second entry that opened into the hall. If she could get that far, she could get free.

She was accustomed to the darkness, and she could see the silver glitter of Michael's eyes as he watched her.

"Yes, it would make things very easy if I'd just *tell* you, wouldn't it?" She laughed, a pleasureless sound that seemed hollow in this shadowy and haunted room. "Then you wouldn't have to do any work at all!"

The glitter shifted, and she suspected he smiled. "I won't have to do much anyway, Jennie," he said. "It's a simple job."

She took two quiet steps, past the chair. "Good, then maybe you can handle it," she said.

He tsked, chastising her, but she ignored the sound. She didn't care if he felt insulted. Why should she hurt so much and he not at all? She needed to get away from him, from the memories—good and bad—that the very smell of him seemed to stir.

In her angry haste she bumped her shin on the low table and with a low cry she reached down and rubbed at the sharp pain.

To her surprise, she heard him chuckle softly, and then an amber light slanted into the room.

"Wouldn't it be easier to go out this way?" He was holding the door open, and suddenly she felt like a fool, caught sneaking toward the bathroom door like the heroine in a hokey spy movie.

"Did you think I planned to lock you up in here and beat you with a rubber hose until you confessed all?" He tilted his head, catching the light along one high cheekbone. Hoping the room was still dim enough to hide her embarrassed flush, Jennie returned to the hall door with as much dignity as she could muster.

He hadn't completely moved from the doorway, and his body was angled so that she had to brush against him to get through.

"Actually I didn't even bring my rubber hose with me," he said as their faces came within a breath of one another. "Your father thought maybe, just maybe, you would tell me on your own."

Jennie felt anger rising like steam inside her. So that was why Michael Winters had been picked for this job! She had assumed her father was calling in a debt. Michael had become a big-time private detective, but he still owed the Kearney family, owed them so much that he could never repay them, no matter how many little "services" he agreed to perform for Arthur.

But now she saw it was more than that. In the old days, her father had teased her mercilessly about her crush on Michael. Arthur had an eagle's eye for people's weaknesses, and he had zeroed in on Jennie's immediately. And now he thought he could use it. He thought that dumb little Jennie would just melt in big, strong Michael's arms and tell him all her girlish secrets.

Well, her father was wrong. He had a lot to learn about little Jennie. And so, apparently, did Michael Winters.

She lifted her chin and looked into his deep brown eyes with a gaze of iron. He'd have a hard time finding any remnant of that young, infatuated Jennie now.

"Tell my father," she said, enunciating carefully, "that he miscalculated. And you—" she ran her gaze down his torso and back up to his eyes "—you'd better send for your rubber hose."

EXHAUSTION WAS NEVER an acceptable excuse for being late for breakfast at the Triple K. So, though she hadn't slept at all, at eight o'clock Jennie forced herself downstairs. She'd gone a bit heavy on the blusher, just in case. A *bit* heavy? She was a walking cosmetics ad, but she'd be darned if she'd let Michael know she hadn't slept all night.

She arrived before her father, but only barely. She had just enough time to fortify herself with a swig of orange juice before he appeared at the French doors, his arrival heralded by his usual fuming. Seven weeks after his stroke, Arthur Kearney still didn't accept the role of invalid gracefully.

Making mollifying noises that only annoyed him further, his nurse settled him in his usual corner of the long back patio, with his usual morning tray of pancakes and coffee beside him.

"For God's sake, hurry up," he barked at the poor woman. "I can't eat stone-cold food."

Watching the nurse's young face blanch, Jennie bit back a protest. Really, her father was an awful tyrant! They'd been through four nurses in the past seven weeks, and it looked as if they might need number five soon.

"That's why they call them *hot* cakes," her father was muttering. "Because they're supposed to be eaten hot."

Now the nurse flushed, but she didn't speak. A surge of anger roiled through Jennie, and she had to clench her teeth tightly to avoid saying something rash. Though she was already furious enough with her father to scream, she knew from years of watching Clare and Quinn tangle with him that opposition only stoked his ire. She had learned to take a more circuitous, but ultimately more successful, route to peace.

"Dad," she broke in calmly, holding up the notebook she always brought down to these morning sessions. "You said you had some important letters to do today. Shouldn't we get started?"

"Did I?" He glowered at her a moment, then nodded with the squint-eyed satisfaction of a tyrant remembering he had a pleasant treat in store. "Oh, right. That doormat Diefendorfer. I was going to fire his incompetent ass, wasn't I?"

"Were you?" she inquired innocently.

"You bet," he confirmed with gusto. Waving the nurse aside, he attacked his pancakes with pleasure. She faded into the background, throwing Jennie a grateful look, and Jennie dared a quick smile in response.

"Okay, here we go." He took a gulp of scalding coffee without even blinking. "Mr. Howard Diefendorfer, et cetera, et cetera. Forget the 'dear Howard' part. Just say— damn it Diefendorfer, how the hell could you lose the school system account for the entire state of Montana? If you can't get the damned account back in twenty-four hours, pack up and get the hell out of Kearneyco. I don't need losers, but I do need Montana."

He popped the last bit of pancake into his mouth and chewed complacently. "Okay. Read that back."

Jennie set her pen down carefully. "Dear Howard," she began, refusing to look up even when her father sputtered over his coffee. "I was distressed to hear that Montana plans to choose another software supplier this year. I trust that you are working to rectify the situation. Please try to resolve this within two weeks. I'll expect your report back then."

A thundering silence fell over the patio. Even the nurse, hovering against the wall of the house, seemed to stop breathing. Off in the distance Jennie could hear a horse's hooves thudding across the rain-soaked pasture. Her heart seemed to keep time with the erratic cantering beat.

Finally she looked up. "Sincerely, Arthur Kearney," she finished, relieved that her voice betrayed none of her internal tumult. "President, Kearneyco."

With effort she met her father's icy blue gaze. This wasn't the first time she had edited his words, and she knew his reaction could go either way, depending on his mood. If he was feeling feisty or frustrated, he could bring the patio roof down with his fury. If he was feeling mellow, he might simply laugh and tease her about having a soft streak just like her mother.

Unfortunately, she saw no signs of amusement this morning. His jaw grew tighter and his eyes grew colder, and she knew he was searching for the right words to pulverize her defiance. Her heart tightened, its pace accelerating to a gallop. She hated these scenes, hated his violent disapproval, and would have done anything to avoid them—anything, that is, except abandon Howard Diefendorfer, a hard-working man who had three children.

But suddenly the anger ebbed from Arthur Kearney's eyes, replaced by a surprising smirk of satisfaction. Braced for a verbal thrashing, Jennie was stunned by the transformation until she realized someone else had joined them on the patio. Michael Winters, looking cool and handsome in an expensive smoky gray business suit, was heading for the buffet table, oblivious to the storm he had interrupted.

Not just interrupted, she realized. Dissipated. Arthur Kearney had begun to chuckle, and Jennie knew why. He didn't really care about Howard Diefendorfer—that was just an insignificant skirmish that he would gladly cede to Jennie. Locating Clare was the real war. And Arthur Kearney clearly believed that Michael was going to win it for him.

"Morning, Winters," he said, still chuckling. "Sleep well?" He watched Jennie out of the corner of his eyes.

"Quite well, sir," Michael said politely, pouring himself a cup of coffee. "And you?"

"Hell, no," Arthur said. "Never do these days. It's living with this thankless child that does it. You know what they say about a thankless child, don't you, Michael?"

"Something about vipers, I think," Michael answered, pulling out a chair and propping his coffee on the wide wooden arm. "But that doesn't sound much like Jennie."

Jennie ignored the smile Michael aimed at her. So he wanted a truce this morning, did he? He wanted to sleep easily in Quinn's bed and then join the family for a chatty poolside breakfast. Oh, yes, he was so at home here, she thought acidly, even after all these years. Just as if he were the son of the house.

But he wasn't. She squeezed the notebook so hard a page ripped free. He wasn't. The son of the house was dead. And this man, who sat in Quinn's chair and munched blithely on a piece of dry toast, was responsible. She mustn't forget that.

"Jennie has been censoring my letters," Arthur went on, obviously enjoying himself. "Her bleeding heart tells her I'm being too rough on one of my employees."

Michael smiled again. "Now that sounds more like Jennie." He tilted his head speculatively. "Is she right?"

Laughing loudly, Arthur slapped Michael's shoulder. "Oh, probably," he said, man-to-man and completely unrepentant.

Man to man. Father to son. The sight drove a lancet of pain through Jennie's chest. Arthur had always been fond of Michael. He had often angrily told Quinn that he should be more like Michael, more conscientious, more responsible. Well, Jennie thought bitterly, when it came down to it, who had been the irresponsible one? And who had paid the price?

Releasing Michael's shoulder, Arthur turned to Jennie. "Say whatever you like. To hell with Diefendorfer. And Montana, too. I'm saving my strength for things that really matter."

His smile broadened, taking on a rather viperish quality of its own. "Like Michael here. His visit matters, and the job he's doing for me matters. And speaking of that, I want you to take him down to Kearneyco and get him settled in. I thought he could use your office, since you're spending most of your time at home now anyway, heading up the letter police."

Jennie opened her mouth, then shut it without speaking. She wouldn't give her father the satisfaction. *Her* office! Whose idea had that been? Had Michael guessed that Clare, afraid to call the ranch, had been getting in touch with Jennie at the office? That must be it. There were plenty of spare desks at Kearneyco. This was just a ruse to cut off any means of safe communication between the sisters.

Her mind sped through the contents of her desk. Had she left any notes that might lead him to Clare? She was so unused to subterfuge. She would have to be very, very careful.

"Spend the day with him," Arthur was continuing. "Introduce him to people. Take him to lunch." He motioned for his nurse. "Dinner, too. I don't want you two out of each other's sights all day." His lips curved in a malicious grin. "Understand?"

"Yes, I do, Dad," Jennie said tightly. "Even better, in fact, than you think."

"Good," he said, propelling the wheelchair toward the French doors so fast the nurse had to lurch forward to open them before he crashed through them. "I like it when people understand me."

CHAPTER THREE

MICHAEL SWALLOWED a yawn and shifted his weight on the leather seat of Jennie's car, letting his foot drop just a tad heavier on the accelerator. The twenty-minute drive into Houston, where the Kearney Building occupied one discreet downtown corner, was going to take about three times that long, if you went by the emotional discomfort clock.

He wondered again why she had insisted they take one car. It had been almost eleven before she'd finally finished taking Arthur's dictation, and, folding her notebook up with a determined snap, she had handed Michael her car keys. "We'll ride together," she'd said firmly. "You drive."

Even at the time he'd been surprised, and now he was downright suspicious. She obviously wasn't motivated by a desire for chitchat. He'd asked a couple of polite questions about changes in the area, but she responded with short yesses and noes, hoarding her syllables like diamonds.

After two or three tries, he gave up. Sooner or later they were going to have to talk, but right now he was too damn tired for games. He concentrated on driving and on keeping his eyes open, which wasn't easy. He'd lied to Arthur this morning. He had definitely *not* slept well.

God, what a night! Memories lurked in every corner of that room, and sleep had been nearly impossible. Quinn's clothes were still in the closet, for God's sake. When Michael had opened the closet door, Quinn's cologne had rushed out at him, tackling him with such force that he could hardly breathe.

And then Jennie had come to him, smelling like roses, looking like heaven and sounding like his bitterest enemy. After that he hadn't slept at all.

"So. I heard you got married."

Jennie's surprising words were spoken in a stilted monotone, but they shocked Michael out of his exhausted thoughts. How had she found out? Though his wedding hadn't exactly been hushed up, neither had it been trumpeted in the social columns. No one had been invited, and no one had come. And immediately afterward he'd moved—fled?—to Seattle.

"Yes," he said, giving her a taste of her own monosyllabic medicine. She hadn't cared to chat about the changing countryside, and he didn't care to talk about this.

She was silent a moment, but his thoughts were clamorous. She must have overheard someone talking about it. But who? Arthur hadn't told her—Michael had already checked on that. Arthur had explained, with something that sounded like an apology, that since the night of Quinn's death Jennie had refused to let anyone speak to her of Michael. So who? He racked his brain, though he kept his face still, his breathing even, his relaxed hand dangling over the armrest. Who?

Alex, perhaps? Alex Todd had been the third member of Quinn's doomed private-investigations partnership, a family friend who, like the Kearneys, had been born to the moneyed life. He had never much liked Michael, whom he considered hopelessly stuffy. Alex had been particularly derisive on the subject of shotgun marriages, which he said any fool could avoid if he had a few hundred dollars, a co-operative doctor and a fistful of conciliatory roses.

Ironically, Alex had become a groom not long after Michael. But Alex's wedding had been a champagne affair. He'd married Clare Kearney, who was as attractive as the trust fund her mother had left her. Not a shotgun in sight.

Yes, Michael could imagine the kinds of observations Alex would have offered about Michael's hasty marriage.

But Alex and Clare lived in New York now, where Alex had opened a chain of trendy, fern-filled restaurants, and Arthur had told Michael that the couple didn't get back to Texas much. Funny, wasn't it, how everyone involved in that terrible night had scattered to the far corners of the national map? Everyone but Jennie, that is. Jennie, armed with innocence, had managed to face down the memories. She had learned to coexist, somehow, with the ghosts.

He slanted a glance at her, trying to guess what else she might have overheard, but her profile was stiff and emotionless, as if the words had come from a ventriloquist.

"Married." Her hands clenched and unclenched in her lap, but her profile didn't change. "To the... to Brooke."

From the restrained sarcasm in her voice he knew what she had been about to say. Married to Brooke the Beautiful Bimbo. Quinn and Alex had dubbed her that, and Jennie, whose sheltered shyness had been so at odds with Brooke's more primal effervescence, had picked it up. The seventeen-year-old Jennie had been transparently jealous of Brooke.

The Beautiful Bimbo. He was glad Jennie hadn't said those words, that her good breeding had asserted itself. Brooke...

His throat tightened uncomfortably, and for a craven moment he wondered what Jennie would do if he simply didn't answer her. Would she ask again? Or would she let it drop, keeping her eyes fixed dully on the road, which shimmered in the heat like an oily river? Perhaps, if he pretended he hadn't heard, the question would ebb away, drifting off on the hot summer breeze.

But he pushed the temptation from him. He had to answer. He wasn't, surely, that much of a coward.

"Yes," he said without turning his head, pretending an intense concern about the car in front of him. "To Brooke."

"So it was true," Jennie murmured, as if to herself. And then she looked up, her voice sharpening. "Where is your wife right now?" A tinny emphasis on the word "wife." "What does she think of your gallivanting off to Texas without her?"

To his surprise, he couldn't answer immediately. A sharp claw of pain pricked at his chest, and he stiffened against it. It was nothing like the savage anguish that had once torn him to shreds, but it was enough to remind him the pain was still there, waiting for him to let his guard down.

"Brooke is dead, Jennie," he said quietly, breathing shallowly until the discomfort subsided. "She was in a car accident."

Jennie gasped, and her face paled, turning an eggshell white, leaving behind two delicate swaths of pink blusher. She looked directly at him for the first time since they got in the car, and her blue eyes were shocked. Apparently she had *not* known, which was the way it should be. Probably no one in Texas knew it, except Arthur, whom Michael had told last night.

Hoping that he and Brooke could start over in Seattle with some chance of building an untainted life, Michael had severed all connections with the Kearneys—and with Alex, with Texas, with anything that would remind him of Quinn. He had, in his desperation, half believed that he could sever the memories, too. What a fool he had been! Guilt didn't recognize state lines.

"Oh, Michael, I'm sorry. I didn't know." He saw her hand move, as if she felt an impulse to reach over and touch him. His arm tingled, anticipating the warmth of her fingers. But she didn't do it. The hand drifted back to her lap.

"I'm so sorry," she said again, and because she was Jennie he could almost believe it might be true. Sorry even for him, though he had no right to her pity. "When did it happen?"

"A long time ago," he said, pushing the car beyond the speed limit. Would they never get to the city? "Almost six years."

She had turned her face to the road, but from the corner of his eyes he saw her brow furrow. "That long?" She sounded confused. "Then—then you must have been married only—"

"Four months," he broke in. Actually it had been four months, two weeks, three days and eleven hours. Not long. Not long enough to get used to sharing a bathroom with Brooke or take for granted the sight of her dresses in his closet.

The claw dug deeper. It hadn't even been long enough to learn to love her.

"But that was just a few months after—" Jennie swallowed audibly "—after Quinn."

He nodded slowly, remembering how difficult it had been, finally climbing out of his despair, his guilt over Quinn's death, only to be knocked right back down into that black pit by Brooke's death. A one-two punch that had nearly knocked the life out of him.

"It was a bad year," he said, hoping he sounded calmer than he felt. He wouldn't let his voice reveal how dreadful it had been. No other soul on earth knew of that long, shadowy month during which he had lost himself.

A whole month. Thirty desperate days that disappeared in sodden hours of unnatural sleep. Thirty nights of phantasmagoric horrors induced by guilt and grief and gin. He had thought he wouldn't survive it—*hoped,* during the worst hours, he wouldn't. But he had, somehow, and as he put his life back together he'd vowed that no one would ever know what a near miss it had been. Least of all Jennifer Kearney.

She must have heard something in his voice, though, because when he turned she was staring at him.

Her fingers were white in her lap, and her eyes held a damp sparkle and a question. "I guess I didn't realize that you cared so much for Brooke," she said slowly. "I knew you—" This seemed hard for her, but she didn't give up. She cleared her throat and went on, as if facing down an enemy.

"I knew there was, well, sex. I wasn't *that* naive. I knew that you…slept with her." She flushed. "But I didn't know that you…loved her."

His heart was suddenly knocking against his rib cage, and his palms were slippery on the steering wheel. Sex. Love. Oh, Jennie, darlin', an inner voice cried, don't ask.

Sex. Love. What could he say about those two tiny words, words that could tangle themselves around your heart, your life, your soul, tying you into knots so twisted you could never get loose? Words that were supposed to be two halves of one satisfying whole, but which were sometimes just jagged pieces of an unsolvable puzzle. Words that could even be the steel jaws of a trap that closed around you….

But though her tone and her eyes asked a question, her words didn't, not technically. So he didn't answer. How could he? She would never understand. He didn't understand it himself.

Instead he gazed out the window and watched as a blur of wildflowers washed by under the huge, cloudless sky. His thoughts were confused, as unfocused as the flowers, merely a jumble of painful impressions. Brooke. Jennie. Quinn. And, as the backdrop to all of it, Texas.

Texas…so big, so hot and ripe and sweet. Living all these years in the foggy hills of Seattle, he had let thoughts of Texas, of home, become something of an obsession. He had let himself believe that, somewhere in these endless spaces, in a field of buttercups or in a whispering forest of loblolly pines, he might someday find the absolution he needed.

Someday. He glanced at Jennie, who still stared at him, her lips compressed, her eyes dry now and hardening as she realized that he had no intention of answering her. She obviously thought she knew what his silence meant, and her brief moment of pity had died.

Absolution? He allowed himself a bitter internal laugh at his own naïveté.

Someday, maybe. But not today.

They finally arrived at the Kearney Building, though for a while Houston seemed like a mirage, always beyond his grasp. He didn't speak another word, and neither did Jennie, until she was forced to part with a few syllables to guide him to her parking space in the cavernous underground lot.

The drive must have seemed overlong to her, too. Before he had quite killed the motor, Jennie whisked out of the car like a submerged swimmer shooting to the surface for air and strode toward the elevator, never once looking around to see if he was following.

He didn't mind. He was used to this role, and her silence was easier to take than her questions. Besides, it gave him time to lock all those painful memories in cold storage where they belonged. Finally he felt his emotions steadying, and he breathed a sigh of relief. He wasn't here seeking absolution or pity, and he wasn't here to relive the past. He had a job to do, and that was all.

The elevator arrived, and they both stepped inside, staring steadfastly at the blank walls, two strangers sharing nothing but the ride. At the third floor she got out and, like the paid shadow he was, he followed a pace or two behind.

Finally they reached double glass doors, which were marked Educational Software, and he could almost hear her breathe a thankful sigh as she shoved them open.

Last night Arthur had proudly informed him that Jennie was head of this division, an important part of the Kearneyco computer empire, but even so Michael was surprised to see what a large department it was. At least fifty desks filled the open central area and ten private offices lined the outer walls.

"Oh, Miss Kearney, thank goodness you're here!" A plump young woman whose glasses seemed to be slightly cockeyed came racing up to Jennie, waving a fistful of pink phone messages. "It's Mr. Faith, the CEO at Barker Enterprises. He says the language is incompatible! He's very upset. It's just awful."

Again Michael was impressed—Jennie was superb. She eased the messages calmly from the woman's fist. "Thanks, Stephanie. I'll call him. What a rough morning you must have had, with him breathing down your neck every hour. He's like that, isn't he? And probably his programmers have just created some small glitch that we can work out in two minutes." She smiled, commiserating and soothing all at once. "Any chance you could get me a cup of coffee? A little caffeine might help me deal with him."

"Can do, boss." Stephanie grinned, her agitated flush fading as she passed her troubles to Jennie with transparent relief and turned her attention to a chore she could handle. Coffee. Adjusting her glasses, she glanced at Michael.

Jennie understood. "Two cups," she amended smoothly, but she didn't answer the question in Stephanie's eyes, and with only a hint of disappointment the secretary scurried off obediently.

Watching Jennie scan the messages and then toss all but one of them into the nearest trash bin, Michael had to smile. God, she was cool! Could this really be the same girl who'd wailed as if her heart would break because she'd developed a blemish on prom night?

They made their way toward her office, but their progress was slow. Everyone wanted to talk to her—since her father's stroke she'd been coming in only once a week, Michael gathered, and that wasn't quite enough.

Blatantly disregarding her father's instructions, she didn't introduce Michael to anyone, not even to the women who ogled him the most openly, begging with their eyes for an introduction.

But if Jennie intended to make him uncomfortable, she failed. He didn't need to meet any of these people—the most curvaceous flirt didn't even remotely intrigue him. His interest was in Jennie alone, and he had ample opportunity to study her as she made her way through the maze of desks toward her office.

She walked in, settled herself behind a large mahogany desk and started flipping quickly through the papers piled there, ignoring him. Leaning on the door jamb, he studied the office. It was charming, businesslike but feminine, with an elegantly upholstered sofa at one end. She looked completely at home here.

Suddenly he realized that, for six years now, he had been stuck in a time warp, remembering Jennie as she had been at seventeen, not taking into account all that had happened since.

And that meant he was going to have to rethink his game plan. He hadn't really taken this job very seriously. Surely, he'd thought, he could either convince Jennie that she must confide in him or, if her resentment ran too deep for that, he could follow her easily to Clare's hiding place. A day or two at the most was all he'd estimated it would take. Jennie was too innocent to hide her secrets well.

Even her steely anger last night hadn't daunted him. He had felt her body's response when he held her against the door, and the man in him had known, without a doubt, that she was still attracted to him, though she might not admit it even to herself.

But here, in her office, in her element, suddenly he saw how foolishly smug that attitude had been. She wasn't a kid any longer, and if her body instinctively yearned for him, well, her mind was quite tough enough to control it.

A curious ache tightened his chest as he watched her. Her face was so serious, her hands so efficient as they sorted papers, her body so poised and lovely in the light that poured over her from the picture window.

The ache grew. As much as he admired this intelligent young woman, he was going to miss that darling, scatty teenager whose emotions had been so near the surface.

Things were buried a bit deeper these days, he guessed. Not that he intended to let that stop him.

"Mind if I sit down?" He didn't wait for her answer. He appropriated the nearest chair and got comfortable, ignoring her swift glance of annoyance.

Yes, much deeper. Time to start digging.

CHAPTER FOUR

IT WAS ALL Jennie could do to keep her fingers from shaking as she searched frantically through the stacks of paper that had accumulated on her desk during the past weeks. Somewhere in this chaos was a pink slip with the phone number for the Stewart's Roost cottage written on it. She had to find it quickly, before Michael realized what she was looking for.

But where was it? Dozens of pink memos taunted her, and she cursed her chronic disorganization. Knowing that Michael was standing in the doorway watching her with an infuriatingly superior smile on his face didn't make it any easier. She had to force herself not to look at him.

When he sauntered casually into the office and took a chair, a sense of panic overwhelmed her, squeezing her chest and stealing her breath. He was going to make this impossible, wasn't he? He wasn't going to give her a moment's privacy. She would never get out to the island today.

Suddenly she desperately wished she were older, braver, full of clever ideas about how to elude his watchful eyes. Clare could do it, if she were the one sitting here. Clare had been born sassy and street smart, not meek and mousy like Jennie.

But she couldn't even think of anything scathing to say, much less anything to *do*. So she clamped down on her nerves and forced her face into a studied neutrality.

He didn't speak, either, but she could feel his gaze on her, as palpable as a touch, raising a light but distracting tingle across her hairline. Pressing a fingertip to her forehead, she discovered to her shame that it was the prickle of perspiration.

Disgusted, she rested her head on her knuckles. This was hopeless. Michael hadn't uttered a word, was, in fact, rather calmly inspecting the crease in his trousers, and already she was breaking out in a sweat. A cold, cowardly sweat.

And then two things, two miraculous pieces of good luck, happened at once. The sought-after memo floated suddenly to the top of the pile, and a voice boomed from the doorway, creating just enough distraction for Jennie to wad the paper up quickly into her clammy palm.

"'See how she leans her cheek upon her hand.'" The voice from the doorway had the deep resonance of an actor. "'Oh, that I were a glove upon that hand, that I might touch that cheek!'"

"Brad?" Slipping the crumpled memo into her skirt pocket, Jennifer rose and moved to the doorway to greet the giant of a man who stood smiling at her, showing large white teeth nestled inside a wild gray-brown beard.

"This is a nice surprise!" She hugged Brad McIntosh tightly. Too tightly, perhaps—she sensed his momentary bemused hesitation before he returned the embrace. Though she'd always been very fond of Brad, he probably couldn't remember her ever being *quite* this happy to see him.

Pulling back, she smiled at him, patting his navy blazer. He had dressed up for this visit. Loyally she tried not to notice how ill at ease he looked in his finery—tried not to compare it to Michael's lazy elegance. It didn't mean a thing. It was just that Brad was more at home in old sweaters and baggy jeans. Nothing wrong with that. Brad was a fascinating man. If she wanted mere sartorial splendor, she might as well date a mannequin. Not that she and Brad were dating, but...

Oh, for heaven's sake! Hearing the jumbled, protest-too-much quality of her thoughts, she told herself to shut up and concentrated on making Brad welcome. "It's great to see you," she said. "I didn't know you were coming in today."

"Ah, my rare and radiant maiden, how could you know anything that goes on around here? You're never here anymore." There was a scold in Brad's tone, but a twinkle in his blue eyes. "Our project has been sadly neglected. I must tell your father you can't be his handmaiden and my muse at the same time."

Jennie groaned, laughing. "Better not put it to him that way," she warned. "Father wouldn't keep a muse on his payroll any more than he would hire the Easter Bunny. Officially I'm your technical adviser."

Brad shuddered visibly. "Technical advis—ugh! No, no, no! Be my muse, my inspiration, my Jennie." He took both her hands and pulled them to his massive chest. "As Keats once said—"

A small noise from the office interrupted what had promised to be one of Brad's more eloquent moments. Jennie couldn't have said whether the sound was a chuckle, a snort or perhaps just Michael shifting in his chair, but it had the effect of making the pair in the doorway whirl around and stare stupidly at him.

Michael's eyes held a hint of wry amusement. Probably a snort, Jennie decided, the indelicate result of swallowing a contemptuous guffaw. Damn his superior hide, she thought, instinctively borrowing one of her father's expressions. He looked as uncomfortably full of secret laughter as an altar boy who'd just heard a traveling salesman joke in church.

Inexplicably embarrassed, she eased her hands free of Brad's grasp. Damn it, though, she told herself, who was Michael Winters to laugh at Brad? Brad was a terrific guy, smart and sensitive and clever, and if he had this one peculiar habit of talking in quotations, well...

"Sorry," Brad said, smiling. He cocked his head and, finding his ear beneath his longish brown hair, tugged on it. "I didn't know you had company."

Jennie looked toward Michael, who had risen, awaiting an introduction, which she realized self-consciously was long overdue. Her back stiffened. Why should she care? She had warned Michael that he wasn't welcome here. Was the prisoner under some social obligation to be polite to her jailer?

But refusing to introduce him seemed childish. "Michael Winters," she said, "I'd like you to meet Brad McIntosh. Brad teaches poetry at SMU. He's helping Kearneyco write a computer program to teach Shakespeare to high school kids."

Michael sauntered over, hand outstretched, and when the two men were side by side Jennie realized that Michael was the first person she'd ever seen who wasn't dwarfed by Brad, either literally or figuratively. Both were tall—about six foot three—but next to Michael's tightly harnessed power Brad seemed messy and disjointed, like a sleepy bear.

"Shakespeare to teenagers? A formidable undertaking," Michael observed dryly as he shook Brad's hand. "I've always admired optimists."

"Yeah," Brad said, pumping Michael's hand. "Well, we're using lots of pictures. The duel in *Hamlet* works particularly well in computer graphics."

"Kind of a Terminator in tights?" Michael's smile was infectious, and Brad rumbled with appreciative laughter.

"Exactly. We're even thinking of having an interactive duel, where the kids can choose to be Hamlet or Laertes. But if they change the ending they have to write a new one. In iambic pentameter, of course."

Jennie watched them, mesmerized. She had hated Michael for so long that she had completely forgotten how charming he could be.

Brad hadn't even told her about this. Michael's interested comments were like a magnet, drawing the information out of the other man. Just as they had once drawn confidences from a sixteen-year-old girl with boy problems.

And then Michael laughed. Just a chuckle, really, but it was the first completely natural laughter Jennie had heard from him since his arrival. It was wonderful—low, mellow tones that curled around her like wood smoke and warmed her like sunshine. She shut her eyes, feeling it, bathing in the painful familiarity of the sound. Oh, how the three of them, she, Michael and Quinn, had laughed together once!

"So come with us," Jennie suddenly heard Brad saying, and she pulled her drifting thoughts together with a jerk. "I was just about to abduct Jennie and make her take me to a perpetual feast of nectar'd sweets. On Kearneyco's tab, of course. We college professors can only afford to feast on egg sandwiches and the occasional Twinkie."

Jennie spotted her chance for escape immediately, like a cornered mouse spotting a hole. Would it work? No, Michael would never fall for it. But she thought of Clare sitting at that grimy window, watching for Jennie's car to pull up, waiting, trusting...and she knew she had to try. Her heart lurched with trepidation as she decided to risk it.

"Oh, I know Michael would love to, Brad," she said, hoping her mouth wasn't too dry to get all the words out, "but he won't be able to spare the time for a leisurely feast today." For safety's sake, she kept her gaze fastened on Brad, not wanting to know whether Michael realized what was coming. This was her best, her only chance, and she had to take it.

"Michael has a lot of work to do," she rushed on, as if the words were blown out of her body by a gust of fear. "Father's hired him for some hush-hush corporate espionage, and I know he's eager to get started." Summoning all her courage, she turned and met Michael's quizzical gaze. "Aren't you?"

Michael's silence probably lasted only a second or two, but to Jennie it seemed to go on for hours. Their eyes locked, brown on blue, power against defiance, amusement meeting fear. But, though her insides were quietly working themselves into tangled knots, she didn't back down. *I dare you,* she said with her eyes, and with the subtle lift of her chin. *I dare you to admit you don't have any work to do here at all.*

Then, to her astonishment, he grinned. "I'm afraid she's right," Michael said smoothly, turning to Brad. "Much as I'd love to go, I'd better stay here and get started."

Looking disappointed, Brad began to protest, but Jennie hushed him and grabbed her purse before Michael could foil her plans. Though she carefully kept any hint of gloating from her expression, she did feel ridiculously pleased that she had been able to devise and execute such a coup. Even Clare, with all her wiles, couldn't have done better than this.

"Let's take my car," she said to Brad as she took his arm. Then, with a false show of concern, she cast a solicitous glance at Michael. "I know that leaves you here without transportation," she said sweetly, "but Stephanie will call a cab when you're finished for the day. Bill our account."

To her surprise, Michael didn't offer a single protest, though surely he could see he'd been outmaneuvered. Although she knew it wasn't ladylike, she couldn't resist rubbing it in just a little.

"Oh, and I may be late," she added casually, adjusting her purse on her shoulder. "If I don't make it home for dinner, will you apologize to Father for me?"

By now he *must* be angry. She watched, searching for signs of smoldering resentment. But she saw nothing of the kind.

"Why, I'd be glad to," he said, his voice losing its newly acquired Northwestern crispness and lapsing into the lazily accommodating, anything-to-please-a-lady drawl of a well-bred Texas gentleman.

Too accommodating. Her complacent triumph began to fade. Much, much too accommodating.

He stood in the doorway as she followed Brad down the hall. Her stomach tightened with every step, and her neck ached from repressing the urge to turn around.

Something was wrong with this picture. Why hadn't Michael looked defeated? Or, if defeat was too much to ask of the great Michael Winters, why not even a little bit put out?

Instead he'd looked... He'd looked sort of... Maddeningly, she couldn't think of the right word.

But just as she and Brad stepped aboard the elevator and the doors closed behind them with a cheerful ding, she caught another glimpse of Michael's face. And she knew, with a flash of awareness that went straight to the pit of her stomach, what the right word was. *Self-satisfied.* He looked amused and thoroughly pleased with himself, like that mischievous altar boy, chock-full of swallowed laughter.

Which meant, of course, that she was in big trouble.

As soon as the elevator closed, Michael shut Jennie's office door and headed for the stairs, jingling the keys that had been hiding in his trouser pocket all morning, a little bundle of insurance lying reassuringly against his thigh.

He loped down the three flights to street level, not needing to hurry. Poor Jennie. Had she really thought to thwart him so easily, as if this was one of those late-night Monopoly games that they used to play? Take that, she'd say, wrinkling her nose. You're stuck on Baltic, and I'm headed for Boardwalk!

This time, though, she had miscalculated. Even though he hadn't tailed anyone in several years—these days he sat behind a desk courting corporate clients while a staff of PIs did the street jobs for him—he hadn't forgotten how. If Jennie had suddenly hopped aboard a rooftop helicopter she might have stumped him, but he sure as hell wasn't rusty enough to get caught without a car.

Before he'd driven to the Triple K last night, he'd left an inconspicuous gray rental sedan parked outside the Kearneyco building, just in case. Just in case—the three most crucial words in the PI's vocabulary. Any detective who didn't live by those three words didn't live long.

Take this business with Clare. On the face of it, nothing special. Only a little domestic wrangle, the kind he avoided like the plague, a job he never would have accepted from any man on earth but Arthur Kearney. Odds were high that Clare was simply indulging in a fit of pique. Clare, Michael remembered, was like that. But Michael had learned long ago that even the sunniest hearts had shadowy corners, and that it might possibly be something more. Something darker.

He quickened his pace, his legs eating up the steps. He had to get to his car first. Just in case.

Luck was with him. He was safely ensconced behind the wheel of his rental car long before Jennie's little coupe stuck its nose cautiously out of the parking garage. Jennie looked both ways, up and down the crowded city street. Her earlier smugness was gone, replaced by a worried frown between her pretty eyes and a white-knuckled grip on the steering wheel.

Michael slouched in the seat, resting his head on his hand, obscuring his profile but positioning himself where he could see her clearly from his rearview mirror. Brad was, of course, still talking, gesticulating with both hands, but Michael doubted that Jennie was hearing a word of it. She looked pale, her blue eyes big and dark in her face.

"Hey, lady! Move it!" The driver behind her leaned on his horn, and as if she'd been stung, Jennie lurched into traffic. Michael tucked himself closer into the seat as she neared him, but her gaze was glued on the main entrance of Kearneyco. She probably expected him to come bolting out and go sprinting through the streets after her.

She never even noticed him. When she was several lengths ahead, he started his motor, checked his rearview mirror and merged quietly into traffic.

Downtown Houston at lunch hour was perfect for tailing, traffic heavy enough to offer camouflage but still maneuverable. Jennie's red coupe was a PI's dream, just expensive enough to be conspicuous, its gleaming paint catching the sun like a spotlight. So even though she was deliberately trying to throw off anyone following her, making abrupt turns and doubling back on herself, it was child's play to keep up.

After a few minutes, Michael had to smile. Most of Jennie's tricks seemed to have come from TV, and the kid didn't have an ounce of killer instinct in her. He laughed out loud when, as the signal switched to yellow, her brake lights blinked on. Obedient Jennie. She couldn't even run a stoplight.

As she waited for the light to turn to green, she craned her neck to look around, but her gaze never lit on the boring gray sedan idling some five car lengths behind. When the light changed, and she sped away, Michael followed easily, settling in to the rhythm of her driving, so attuned he could almost predict which way she would turn and when.

His gaze was locked on Jennie's car when suddenly the world seemed to lunge forward, blurring his focus and knocking the breath out of him. As if in slow motion, he felt the steering column try to knock a hole through his rib cage, felt his head whip toward the windshield and then back as the seat belt grabbed his shoulder.

What the hell? Slamming on the brakes, he swerved to avoid the car in front of him and, thank God, brought the sedan to a safe stop on the easement, though his pulse raced and his chest was aching in circles of pain. Fighting to capture his breath, his gaze flew to the mirror.

It was like a scene from a surreal comedy film. Small navy blue gremlins were swarming out of a minivan, laughing gremlins and screaming gremlins—surely more than the van could possibly have held, Michael thought numbly as he reached for the ignition key. *Turn off the engine,* he told himself, fighting the urge to hit the accelerator and shoot off after Jennie, whose red car was already two blocks down the street.

"Damn!" He ran his hand through his hair, breathing deeply, and checked the rearview mirror again. The gremlins—which, as his confusion subsided, were resolving themselves into about a dozen kids dressed in Boy Scout blue—were clustering around the one adult-size figure in the tableau, clamoring excitedly. Some were crying, but they all looked intact. "Damn," he muttered again, watching as Jennie's car diminished to a dot of sunlight that winked and finally disappeared. What a mess!

"You okay, mister?"

Michael started at the sound, high and sweet, of a young boy's voice at his window. He turned—slowly, because he wasn't quite sure his neck wasn't broken—and met his inquisitor.

It was one of the gremlins, about four feet tall, bone-skinny, and with a look of mischief in his speckled brown eyes that utterly belied the soprano sweetness of his voice. This little gremlin obviously thought a car accident was a major-league thrill.

"You okay?" the boy repeated, and Michael realized that, ghoulishly, the kid was almost hoping he wasn't. Typical six-year-old, he thought, and then caught himself up short. How in hell would he know anything about six-year-olds? He hadn't spent a day, not one single goddamn day, as a father.

He tried to smile, but sickeningly, he couldn't. He tried to speak, but no words came. Oh, God. He swallowed hard. It hadn't happened in a long time, this frozen paralysis in the presence of children. For the first few years it had been relentless. Especially around little boys. Especially little boys who were the age his own son would have been if—

His son would have been five now. Would he have looked like this? Would he have had freckles sprinkled under his eyes, like a spill of pepper? Would his smile have been so crooked? Would his teeth have looked like an unfinished jigsaw puzzle, with an empty square in the center? Would he have had a perpetual smudge across his cheek and grubby hands, amazing hands, so small and yet so perfect, so full of curiosity, unaware of being little...

"Yeah, I'm okay," Michael said, sucking in the pain hard and swallowing it down, pushing it deeper this time, deep enough to stay down.

The kid was frowning dubiously, and Michael knew he must appear strange. His head was light, as if all the blood had drained out through an invisible wound. He could feel sweat standing on his forehead, and his eyes were wet, making the world look like crushed rainbows.

"Yeah," he lied, more robustly this time. He even managed some semblance of a smile. "Yeah, kid, I'm fine."

AFTER DROPPING BRAD OFF at his house, it took Jennie two hours to make the one-hour trip to Clare's cottage. By the time she got there she was limp with anxiety, but she did finally get there. And, most importantly, she arrived *alone*.

She was pretty sure of that. When she had crossed the rickety bridge to Stewart's Roost, no other car had even been in sight. Once on the island, she was even more confident. The sickly cabbage palms and toothless saw-grass clusters were too anemic to hide a bicycle, much less a car.

Clare was waiting, just as Jennie had pictured her, and opened the door before Jennie's car had come to a full stop. She was wearing the same white nightgown from yesterday, and the sight of the wrinkled cotton made Jennie's heart skip a beat. Elegant Clare, clotheshorse extraordinaire, wearing day-old nighties? The thought was strangely unsettling.

While Jennie gathered groceries and supplies from the back seat, Clare stared down the sandy ruts that served as an access road to the beachside cottage, as if expecting to see a phantom car materialize out of the shimmering heat.

"You're sure no one followed you?" she asked querulously, as though Jennie was a child who couldn't be trusted to get anything right.

Jennie felt herself bristle, but fought the feeling. Clare's face was gray, and her beautiful hair was limp and dull. Jennie couldn't ever remember Clare neglecting herself like this.

"I'm sure," she said, hoisting the last bag in her arm and folding her purse under her chin, the only spot left for holding anything. She bumped the car door shut with her hip. "Clare," she said as evenly as she could without moving her lower jaw, "do you think you could maybe take my purse?"

Clare bustled forward then, apologizing, and grabbed a couple of the grocery bags, as well. "Sorry, Jen," she said as they dumped the supplies on the nicked kitchen counter. "I don't know what's the matter with me. I'm just a wreck sitting out here all alone. I keep waiting for Daddy or Alex or some damn private investigator they've hired to come rapping at my door, ready to drag me back to New York.''

Jennie pulled a six-pack of diet soda from the first bag and slid it onto the refrigerator shelf.

''Well, they won't find you if I can help it,'' she said, adding a quart of orange juice and a package of bologna. The little grocery store at the mouth of the bridge hadn't been big on the gourmet items Clare usually preferred. ''I was so careful today I think I came here by way of Idaho.''

Clare didn't smile. ''Why?'' Her voice was half an octave higher than usual, and she leaned forward to clutch Jennie's forearm. ''Was someone following you?''

Jennie put her hand soothingly over her sister's hot fingers. Clare had an overwrought look, all brittle tension, and Jennie was afraid the news might be more than she could handle. After Quinn's death, Clare had felt as Jennie had, that Michael was to blame. Michael, who should have been with Quinn at the warehouse, protecting him, backing him up, had *not* been there. Instead, Michael had been across town at Brooke's little lovenest, mindlessly seeking cheap thrills while Quinn lay dying. Neither of Quinn's sisters would ever, ever forgive Michael Winters for that.

''Clare, you were right about Dad,'' she admitted softly. ''He has hired someone.''

''I knew it!'' Clare's eyes grew rounder and brighter, and the skin around them looked bruised. ''A detective?''

Jennie nodded. ''And it's even worse. It's not just any detective.'' She clasped Clare's hand tightly, communicating all the strength she could. ''It's Michael Winters.''

Jennie had been prepared for anger, even fury—but not for the reaction she got. Clare stared for a moment, disbelieving. And then she let out a long moaning sound, so low it seemed involuntary.

''Michael Winters,'' Clare whispered, and her fingers trembled on Jennie's arm. Jennie feared for a moment that

Clare might fall—if her legs were as unsteady as her grip, how could they hold her up? She reached out, ready to catch her.

But to her surprise Clare broke away and without another word stumbled toward the bathroom, slamming the door behind her. Jennie stood in the kitchen, trying to make sense of it. Was all this fuss the result of merely hearing Michael's name? Surely not, she thought, bewilderment compounding on itself.

And then she heard, through the paper-thin walls, the unmistakable sounds of Clare being horribly, miserably ill.

Jennie stared at the door, impotent in her pity and confusion. It was such a violent sound—much too extreme a reaction even for Clare. Dread settled like a block of ice in her stomach. Oh, God, what was wrong with Clare?

It seemed, like a nightmare, to go on forever, but finally Jennie heard the sound of flushing and then water splashing in the sink. The door opened slowly and Clare emerged, her scrubbed-clean face still damp and as white as her nightgown. Jennie couldn't quite read her expression—except that it looked lost, caught somewhere between fear and shame.

Suddenly, like a bolt of psychic lightning, the truth hit her. She grabbed hold of the counter to steady herself.

"Clare," she said in a voice she hardly recognized. "Clare, are you pregnant?"

CHAPTER FIVE

AN HOUR LATER they were sitting on low-slung beach chairs, so close to the water's edge that every incoming wave nibbled at their bare toes. Clare might have been asleep. Her head had fallen back, and her eyes were closed tightly against the sun. But the knuckles of her twined hands were pale, and Jennie knew she was wide awake, her mind struggling silently with its demons.

She wished Dad could see Clare now—this silence alone would certainly banish his cynicism. Ordinarily, whenever Clare was out of sorts she was a fountain of complaints, fuming and frothing ceaselessly about the injustices she suffered.

Jennie shivered in the humid afternoon air, wondering what could have wrought such a change. Demons, indeed.

If only Clare would tell Jennie what they were! Jennie was struggling, too, but she was battling with shadows. *Pregnant.* That was the first shadow. Clare was going to have a baby sometime around Christmas, Alex's baby, though he didn't know it, and Clare had sworn he never would. Then, tearfully, had come the second shadow. *Divorce.*

But not a syllable was spoken of *why.* Biting her lip, Jennie watched the gulf heave and roll, as if something monstrous moved beneath its silver-green surface. Anxiety undulated through her mind with the same unformed malevolence. Why? She'd asked a hundred times, with only fresh waves of tears as answer.

"You know, Clare," Jennie said again, unable to bear the silence through which so many unseen enemies moved, "I could really be more help to you if I knew what you were afraid of."

Her voice came out almost a whisper, which was ridiculous. Looking down the beach, she saw only a half a dozen people—a mother supervising a toddler, three kids building a sand castle and an over-baked couple writhing in romantic oblivion. No one lurked about suspiciously; no one was listening or spying.

Annoyed with herself, Jennie stood abruptly, twisting her hair away from her damp neck and sighing. Someone needed a clear head, but, damn it, Clare's paranoia seemed to be contagious.

"Listen, we have to do something. Hiding out here won't make whatever's bothering you go away." Jennie spoke more forcefully now, trying to get Clare to open her eyes. But she didn't. If anything, she squeezed them shut more tightly. "Look, if it's something Alex has done, if it's another woman, we should tell Dad. He'd never want you to put up with infidelity."

No answer, not even a twitch of Clare's firmly pursed lips. So it wasn't another woman. Ironically, Jennie was almost disappointed. Alex as the cheating husband had seemed the most obvious scenario, and somehow the easiest to cope with. There were time-honored rules for dealing with adultery. Now she had the uncomfortable feeling that Clare's dilemma lay in more treacherous, uncharted territory.

Anxiety shifted in Jennie's chest, tripping her heartbeat as she looked at Clare, still sitting passively, as if a spell had been cast over her. Jennie had persuaded her to get dressed, but putting on jeans and a T-shirt hadn't infused her with any life.

"Well, okay, what if we hire a detective ourselves, then?" Jennie dug her toes into the damp sand, finding a mild relief in the cool moisture. "If you're really going to get a divorce, you'll need to protect yourself. You'll need ammunition."

Clare's eyes flew open. "Not Michael. *Never.*"

Jennie stared, mystified by the forceful reaction, especially since mention of their dreaded father hadn't elicited so much as a murmur. "I didn't say *Michael,*" she said placatingly. "There are other detectives. But, actually, now that you mention it, why not Michael? He's going to find you sooner or later, Clare. We'd be safer if we could explain things to him, maybe even get him on our side."

"Not *him.*"

"But *why?*" Jennie pushed her hands through her hair, fighting the urge to pull it out. This was making her crazy. "Because of what happened to Quinn? Michael has changed, Clare. He's hardly an incompetent amateur any more. I think he must be pretty good, actually."

She was sure of that, though she couldn't pinpoint how she knew. Was it the expensive car? Or the finely tailored suits? Maybe it was the way he carried himself, always watching—aware of everything, afraid of nothing.

"He's slick," she finished, unable to describe the changes any more accurately. "In fact, anyone less incompetent than Michael Winters today would be hard to imagine."

"Jennie," Clare said slowly, her eyes staring at the sequined water though her gaze was strangely unfocused, as if she saw nothing, "Jennie, did it ever occur to you that maybe he wasn't incompetent back then, either?"

Jennie frowned, an inch away from real anger. Was Clare changing the subject? Had she even heard a single word?

"What do you mean?"

Maddeningly, Clare didn't answer. She just plucked absently at the knee of her jeans and stared that vacant stare.

"Clare, what?" Jennie plopped onto her beach chair and shook her sister's arm. "What do you mean?"

Clare turned her face slowly toward Jennie. "Just what I said. We always assumed Michael and Quinn bungled that warehouse job. We figured they were too naive, too inexperienced, to realize that they really needed two men on the job at all times. But what if it wasn't a mistake?"

"Wasn't a mistake?" Somewhere in the back of Jennie's mind, Clare's meaning was crackling dangerously, but she couldn't let herself hear it. "What do you mean it wasn't a mistake?" she repeated stupidly. "Do you mean you think it might have been—"

"Deliberate." Clare interjected the word harshly, and her gaze was clear. Clear, and frightened as hell. "I mean it might have been deliberate. Someone might have paid him to get out of the way that night. Did that ever occur to you?"

Appalled nearly to the point of speechlessness, Jennie shook her head. "No. No. *Never!*"

Clare's mouth twisted bitterly. "Michael's got a PI firm now, right? He's a success, a big deal in Seattle?"

"Yes. No. I don't know." Jennie was practically stammering, her heart hammering in her chest. How could Clare be saying these things? How could she even think that Michael— "Not *that* big, really, I mean, I don't know how big...."

"Well, I do. I checked. He's got twenty people on a full-time payroll and God knows how many free-lance operatives working part-time. *And* an uptown address. That's big in my book. Where do you think he got the money for all that?"

Jennie was still shaking her head, as if she could deny the twenty employees, deny the fancy address, though she knew Clare must have researched it. "We knew he got insurance money," she said, hanging onto that one pitiful fact. "We knew that. Alex got his half, too. All the partners were insured, remember? Just in case something happened." She met Clare's eyes, willing her to agree. "It's a common business practice, Clare."

But Clare wasn't interested. She had already turned back to the gulf, and Jennie was irrationally angry at her sister's ability to withdraw from the emotional storm she'd set in motion.

"Damn it, Clare," she said, leaning forward and bringing her voice down to a low-pitched intensity. "Alex got insurance money, too. And he wasn't there that night, was he? Your husband wasn't there to save Quinn, either."

"It wasn't his shift." Surprisingly, Clare sounded defensive, as if Jennie's accusation had hit deep, where loyalty was still rooted. "Michael was supposed to be there, not Alex. Alex had the night off."

"Well, maybe that wasn't coincidence, either," Jennie insisted doggedly. "Why confine your suspicions to Michael? Alex started his restaurants with his half of the insurance money, didn't he? And he has more than a hundred employees now."

If Jennie had been surprised by Clare's show of loyalty, she was even more stunned by her own. Michael was nothing to her, not husband, not lover, not even friend. So why was she so furious with her sister for maligning him?

Perhaps simply because it was so unfair. Michael could never have done such a dreadful thing. Good God, that would mean it was more than negligence, more than carelessness. It would mean murder. Premeditated. Cold-blooded. Murder. As the word formed in her mind, a slow, icy chill dripped down her spine.

"You know everyone suspected the Mitchell family arranged their own robbery," Clare whispered, her gaze darting nervously as if she feared being overheard. "Well, maybe the Mitchells paid Michael and Alex to stay away— to make sure only one guy, one helpless guy, was guarding the warehouse that night."

Paid Michael *and* Alex? Jennie had just barely registered her sister's words when Clare's face crumpled.

"Oh, God, Jennie," Clare said brokenly, and then slowly began to shake her head. She kept it up, like a programmed robot performing a repetitive, meaningless command, until Jennie grabbed her by the shoulders and brought her to a rough halt.

"Stop that!" Jennie's voice was harsh and raw. She didn't want to hurt Clare, but she needed to make her see how outrageous this was. "Listen to me." Her fingers pressed into her sister's upper arms. "Listen to yourself! Can you really believe they were *both* involved? Michael and Alex? Working together, doing something that put Quinn in jeopardy? Is that what you think?"

Clare was shivering, a convulsive shudder that seemed to spring from deep inside her. And then she began to cry.

"I don't know, Jennie," she sobbed, leaning her head against Jennie's collarbone and wrapping her arms around her sister. "Oh, God, I just don't know."

IT WAS ALMOST MIDNIGHT, and there were no signs of life at the Triple K. Trying not to wake anyone, Michael let himself into Quinn's room and threw his jacket across the bed.

Damn, he was tired. Loosening his tie, he dropped onto the chair in front of the desk and tried to summon the energy to check in with his Seattle office. But he made no move to pick up the telephone. He knew, with some sixth sense, that his secretary had nothing to tell him, and he didn't need any more frustrations in this endlessly frustrating day.

The blasted Boy Scouts had been just the beginning. God, what a bad break! It had taken forever. By the time the police were finished checking licenses and writing up the report, Jennie'd had enough time to drive to Tanzania and back.

He'd learned long ago that, in his business, bad luck only bred more bad luck, and today had been no exception. Not a damned thing had gone right. The picture of Jennie that Arthur had given him was pretty good, coming from the personnel office at Kearneyco. But the one of Clare was so blurry it might have been anyone from Greta Garbo to Wilma Flintstone. Arthur Kearney was not a sentimental man with albums full of his kids' pictures. He'd obviously had to scrounge for these.

Still, photos in hand, Michael had checked with a dozen realtors, none of whom remembered ever seeing either woman. Ditto at a dozen hotels and a handful of apartment buildings.

The only promising lead to come out of the day was from the garage that detailed Jennie's car. The spike-haired teen who worked the pumps obviously had a crush on her and was eager to tell everything he knew. Jennie's car had been in more frequently these past two weeks, the kid had said, leering happily. It needed gas about twice as often. And it was sandy, even on the inside, like she'd tracked some in on her shoes.

The beach? But that had been a dead end, too, at least for today. Michael had faxed the photos to hotel security at three or four of the best resorts within driving distance, but the answers had all come back negative. Nobody remembered seeing these women. And, looking at Jennie's smiling picture, Michael couldn't believe that, once seen, she would be forgotten.

With a quiet curse he picked up the telephone and dialed collect to Seattle.

"Winters Investigations." Lisa's voice, even at this hour, was a purebred purr. Michael smiled inwardly, thinking how well his secretary's voice matched her looks—a wow-just-imagine sexuality encased in a don't-even-think-about-it elegance. But he knew the real Lisa, just as Lisa knew the real

Michael. Both of them were smooth on the surface, but they'd grown up in hard places, and they had the calluses to prove it.

They recognized that inner toughness in the other without saying a word, which was why they worked so well together. It was also why they'd always be friends and never lovers.

"Hi," he said, not bothering to try to hide his weariness. Lisa could always see through any phony macho stoicism. "It must be after ten there. Why haven't you gone home yet?"

"Been waiting for you to call, handsome," Lisa said, and he could hear the smile in her voice. "Just sitting here draped over the telephone, pining away."

"Avoiding Ray again, you mean?" Lisa's boyfriend had been getting too serious lately, so Lisa had been putting in a lot of long nights at the office.

"Out of bounds." Lisa starched her voice just a bit. "Listen, handsome, I refuse to be psychoanalyzed over the phone. And by a man who's afraid of a seventeen-year-old girl, no less."

Michael scowled, yanking his tie from his neck. "She's twenty-three, and I'm not afraid of her. And where the hell did you get that idea, anyway?"

Lisa chuckled, low and sexy, obviously pleased with her bull's-eye. "Well, something about Arthur Kearney's phone call sure drained the blood out of your face. I've never seen a man go gray in three seconds flat. So I figured, it can't be the father—men don't make men go gray. And it can't be the missing sister—she's married, more or less, and she's definitely a flake. So it has to be the kid." She paused, as if to let her logic sink in. "Right?"

Michael almost laughed. "God, you fight dirty, you know that? If I officially withdraw the remark about Ray, will you back off?" Without waiting for her answer, he pulled out his notebook and cocked his pen. "Now how about some business? I hope your day was more productive than mine."

"Not much." He heard the rustle of paper as she opened her notebook. "No one has gone within a mile of Clare Todd's credit cards or bank accounts in two weeks. Before that she took out a lot of cash, but that wasn't unusual. She hasn't bought a plane ticket, rented a car, applied for a job or won the lottery. She must be living under the highway and eating cat food by now."

Michael finally did laugh, as Lisa had no doubt intended him to. "Not this lady," he said cynically. "This one is the five-star and caviar type."

"Well, good," Lisa said. "Caviar's easier to trace than cat food." He heard her notebook flip to a new page. Lisa chattered a lot, but she didn't, in the long run, really waste any words. "So. What does tomorrow hold?"

"Let's get a list of all the rentals—particularly short-term rentals—in a fifty-mile radius of Houston. Jennie goes to see Clare, I'm sure of that, but she's always home to sleep in her own bed." He paused for a moment, wondering if Jennie was in that bed right now. Her car had been in the driveway, but it was still warm. And the odometer had jumped up by a hundred miles. Hence the fifty-mile radius.

"And put somebody on Alex Todd," he said, surprising himself. It wasn't a conscious decision—it was just one of those gut instincts. But he had learned long ago—six years ago, to be exact, when his gut had told him to stay at the warehouse with Quinn though an entirely different part of his body was telling him to hightail it over to Brooke's—that ignoring his instincts could be damned dangerous.

"The husband?" Lisa sounded surprised, too.

"Yeah, let's see what he's up to. Maybe he's looking for her. He knows her better than we do—maybe he'll find her first. I want to be there if he does." He rubbed his face with his hand, trying to banish the fuzzy exhaustion that was taking over. "Oh, and Clare's doctor. Get somebody to find out who he is and how recently she's seen him."

"Looking for anything in particular?"

"Black eyes? Bruises? Broken bones?" Michael shook his head wearily. "Alex was an ass, but I never saw any signs of violence in him." He sighed. "Oh, hell, I don't know, Lisa. Maybe Alex got weird. Maybe Clare's got a good reason for running. Jennie has certainly decided I'm the bad guy here. I get the feeling she'd like to ship me back to Seattle in a box."

"See?" Lisa sounded smug as she snapped her notebook shut. "I told you you were afraid of her."

By two in the morning Michael was ready to abandon any idea of sleeping. The full moon had positioned itself so that it shone onto his pillow like the spotlight at a police interrogation. And his stomach was starting to grumble irritably about people who weren't thoughtful enough to eat dinner.

Stopping only to pull an old cutoff Army T-shirt over the soft sweat shorts he was using as pajamas, he headed down the stairs, his mind already building the perfect sandwich. His bare feet were silent on the carpeted steps. He hadn't felt the need to add a robe or shoes—there hadn't been a sound in the house in two hours. Except, of course, from his indignant stomach.

But as he rounded the first landing he noticed the flickering shadows that emanated like restless ghosts from the small den at the back of the house. He had misjudged. Someone else was still awake.

He stopped mid-step, reading the shadows. Not amber enough for a fire, not smooth enough for human movement. Their silvery, jerky dance could come from only one thing—a television showing an old black-and-white movie.

And that, too, could only mean one thing. Jennie. Sweet, silly Jennie, who could watch *Casablanca* a hundred nights straight and cry every time. Jennie, who probably found sleep as elusive tonight as he did.

Without hesitating long enough to change his mind, he headed for the den. And sure enough, there she was, her hair tumbling around her shoulders, a cascade of silver in the half-light.

Judging from her pale face, she wore no makeup at all, or had already cried it all off. A box of tissues sat on the sofa beside her, and the floor was littered with small white clumps. This one must be a real tearjerker, he thought with a sudden rush of affection. What a soft heart she had!

She clearly hadn't expected to see anyone down here tonight. Her sleeveless, long cotton nightgown was designed to be completely sexless, though somehow, on her, it failed. She sat cross-legged on one corner of the sofa, her nightgown hitched up around her thighs, a bowl of popcorn cradled between her knees.

As he watched, she gulped a mouthful of something she had poured into a brandy glass. Not a soft drink, he decided as she swallowed, grimaced and softly coughed, wiping her mouth with the back of her hand.

"Good movie?"

Jennie started, nearly knocking over the popcorn. She clasped the brandy glass to her breast, as if to hide it. No, definitely not a soft drink.

Her gaze darted uncomfortably from the doorway to the television screen. "Yes," she said, but her throat was clogged. She had to clear it and begin again. "It's the original *Jane Eyre*."

Michael glanced at the TV. *Jane Eyre* hadn't ever been one of his favorites—he'd always thought Rochester ought to stop brooding and take his lumps like a man. But he also noticed that the movie was only about halfway over—hardly Kleenex time. So why was Jennie already crying?

"Mind if I watch, too?" Michael didn't wait for an answer. He claimed the empty side of the sofa and grabbed a fistful of popcorn. "Hope you've got plenty of this. I missed dinner."

Jennie pried the bowl from between her knees and placed it carefully between them. Well, the symbolism of *that* was pretty obvious, Michael thought as he took another handful.

Apparently his presence made Jennie uncomfortable. She shrank into her corner like a flower that folds against the night, and she took another liberal sip of her drink. Up close, it looked and smelled a lot like scotch. Her eyes were puffy from crying, but it was too shadowy to see if they were red. Still, he wondered how much she had drunk already.

"So," Jennie said, staring stonily at the television, "why did you miss dinner?"

"I guess I forgot." He stared at the screen, too. He could see her perfectly well in his peripheral vision, just as he knew she could see him. "I was pretty busy."

She darted a glance at him, and even sideways he could tell it was full of contempt. "I bet you were. What do you guys do all day? Snoop around in people's garbage cans? Gee, I'd have thought you might find something for dinner in there."

She must have had plenty of that scotch—she was laying the sarcasm on with a trowel. He decided not to rise to the bait. Munching blithely on another handful of popcorn, he watched Joan Fontaine weep softly, then he answered with good humor.

"Come to think of it, I haven't had a good banana-peel soup in years. Just shows how much I miss now that I don't do trash searches any more."

"Don't you?" Jennie sounded skeptical, and she punctuated her disdain with another sip of scotch. "Are you trying to tell me you can build a detective agency the size of yours without getting a little garbage on your hands?''

The movie had given way to a commercial for a psychic hot line, and the audio was twice as loud as it had been for the film. He had to raise his voice to answer.

''Actually there's not much money in trash these days, Jennie. The guy who wants to know if his wife is sleeping with her tennis pro won't pay much—not compared to the CEO who wants to know if his VP is selling secrets to the other guys.''

And, for a moment, that shut her up. Obviously she knew common sense when she heard it. An uncomfortable silence ensued. The psychic hot line finally gave up trying to get them to call, and the movie returned. Michael began to wish he had a glass of Jennie's scotch. The popcorn was sadistically salty.

''Michael,'' Jennie said abruptly, as if she had made an important decision, though she still didn't take her eyes from the screen, ''let's suppose for a minute that my father is right. That I do know where Clare is.''

He watched her profile, so elegantly drawn and yet so innocent. Against the flickering shadows it looked like a silhouette cut from silver paper. She looked so intense, her little bud of a mouth unsmiling and serious. He had to stop himself from reaching over to touch it.

''Okay,'' he said as somberly as he could manage. ''I guess I can suppose that, just for a minute.''

The quick pursing of her lips told him she had recognized the mild sarcasm, but she didn't acknowledge it with words. ''Okay,'' she went on, placing her glass carefully on the end table. ''Well, if you're following me, I just won't go. You can see that, can't you? So how does that help anyone? Suppose you manage to make it impossible for me to see her. Who will keep her company? Who'll bring her food and money? Who'll take her to the movies, the library, the doctor? Who'll—"

But he didn't let her finish. "Doctor?" He pounced on the word, a small twist of anxiety moving through him. It so closely mirrored his earlier hunch. "Does she need to go to the doctor?"

Jennie turned toward him finally, and her eyes held a stricken look, her mouth opening slightly in dismay. He'd struck a nerve, he could tell, but he didn't feel any joy from the victory. He had wanted to be wrong.

"Is she sick, Jennie?" He modulated his voice, trying to coax the answer out of her the way he might coax a frightened bird onto his finger. "Is she hurt?"

Jennie swallowed, the sound lost in the music swelling from the television, but he saw the slim column of her throat tighten nervously. His heart ached for the confusion and turmoil he saw on her face, and he put his hand on her bare leg, the only part of her he could reach.

"Jennie," he said softly, cupping the warm, silky mound of her knee in the palm of his hand. "You've got to let me help."

CHAPTER SIX

SHE DIDN'T shift away, though he could see in her eyes that she wanted to. The muscles in her leg were clenched, as if she was trying to reject his possession, but a pulse behind her knee beat rapidly under his encircling fingers.

She looked down and swallowed hard again. "Really, Michael," she said, apparently attempting to sound light, but managing only a brittle iciness. "This was strictly hypothetical, remember? There's no need to get so serious."

"Jennie—"

But she wouldn't let him go on. The pulse under his hand accelerated, and she laughed shakily. "Let's talk about something else," she said, finally giving in to her need to escape his touch. She shifted, putting her knees together and pulling her nightgown down as far as it would go. "Tell me more about your work. It must be exciting. Is it awfully dangerous?"

He wasn't sure he could stand it, this switch to vapid debutante chatter. Flatter him, butter him up, ask him about himself and make him feel big and strong. Keep the conversation in safe, shallow ruts so that no one can get too close.

To hell with that! He wanted more. A lot more. He wanted the truth, damn it. He wanted her to trust him enough to lay her heart open, to put her troubles at his feet and let him carry them for a while. He wanted her to believe that he was capable of doing it.

But who was he kidding? Sure, he wanted all those things—but even more than that he wanted to put his hand on her skin again. He wanted to know if her lips were as soft as they used to be. He wanted to know if the bud of sexuality he had glimpsed six years ago had ever blossomed, and if the flower was as intoxicatingly sweet as he had sometimes dreamed it would be.

But all she wanted, damn her indifference, was to maneuver herself out of this awkward moment. He set his jaw and tried to pull himself together.

"Your nose looks different," she was saying. "As if it's been broken. Has it?"

"Yes." His nose and two ribs, by three thugs in an alley. Then again in a St. Louis bar, where he had followed an embezzler, back in the days before the twenty employees, before the suits and the corporate clients. "More than once."

"So it is dangerous, then."

"Sometimes." Maybe it was just because his nerves were on edge, but the conversation annoyed him. She thought this was safe small talk, but that just showed how sheltered she had always been. She was still Daddy's little rich girl, playing at her exciting new game of hide-and-seek. She hadn't a clue, had she? In spite of what had happened to Quinn, Jennie really had no idea how dirt-common cruelty was.

"See that?" He lifted his T-shirt almost angrily. Damn it, he would show her. He would make the conversation real again, no matter how deftly she tried to dance into impersonal chitchat. Danger was about as personal as you can get.

"What?" She peered, tilting her head one whole inch closer to him. Her hair fell over her shoulder in a silver shadow. "No. It's too dark. Where?"

"Here." Before she could protest, he grabbed her hand and guided it to his right side, where an ugly four-inch scar curved below his rib cage, the reminder of a knife wielded by the prettiest secretary he'd ever seen—a secretary who happened to be selling her boss's technical designs to her lover.

He slid her fingers across the rigid scar tissue. "A lady gave me that. She was going for my heart. She had lousy aim."

"Michael..." Even in the dim light he could see the dull flush that darkened Jennie's cheekbones. He had pulled her over suddenly and hard, and in order not to lose her balance, she had to lean her body across the sofa. Her arm stretched across his lap, and her head was at his chest level. At first her fingers were tense, resisting, but as she began to realize what they were touching they grew soft, gentling with a shocked tenderness.

"Oh, Michael," she breathed, and in the words he heard all the understanding he could have hoped for. Her imagination was clearly filling in the blanks, telling her what kind of pain had left such a permanent mark.

He felt a twinge of shame. It was a damned cheap trick, and he knew it. But he couldn't stop himself. He wanted her to touch him, to admit that he was real. He wanted to feel her silky fingers on his skin. He wanted her to come even closer, so that his nose was filled with the smell of scotch and perfume, so that her breasts brushed against his chest. He wanted it so badly he could hardly breathe.

He leaned his head against the back of the sofa, shutting his eyes. Tension gripped him as he waited. Would her fingers move on, beyond the paltry four inches of his scar to the rest of him? Would she know, would she somehow sense, that there were other wounds, other parts of him that had suffered, though no scars marked their presence? Would she sense, with those soft fingertips, how much his very soul ached and cried out for comfort?

And if she did, what would he feel? For six years he had felt an abysmal nothing. Nothing. Guilt and pain had numbed him to all physical pleasure, and though his flesh responded like any man's, his mind, his heart could not participate in the sensations. He was locked away in a prison of his own making.

Her fingers ran the length of the scar time and time again, as if memorizing the size and shape of it. And then, finally, just when he had begun to give up, they moved across his stomach, to the other side, where his skin was smooth and hard.

Muscles rippled in her wake, tightening against the tickling heat of her touch. She traced first the lowest rib, then the next and then the next, until she had reached under his short T-shirt and found the small dark nub of his nipple.

He bit back a groan, afraid that the slightest sound might distract her from her tentative exploration. A familiar tightening was constricting his belly. He had to remind himself to breathe, but with every second it grew more difficult to force air into his lungs.

She put her other hand on him, too, just above his heartbeat, which by now was racing in place. Slowly she lowered her face, and ducking her head as if shy, she pressed her forehead against his chest, her breath quick and warm in the hollow between his ribs.

The tension was so strong—far more akin to pain than pleasure. But he knew what heaven lay beyond the pain, if only he could get there, if only his frozen body would melt under the warmth of her fingers and let the sensations through. He wanted it. Something inside screamed out for it, though only the smallest of sighs escaped his clamped jaws.

Oh, God, yes, please. He wanted to stand beneath a cascade of sensation the way the first man on earth might have stood beneath a roaring waterfall, dumb with amazement, weak with joy, praying in awestruck gratitude.

But then he felt something else, something that had nothing to do with pleasure and everything to do with pain.

He felt the silver burn of a trail of tears. Jennie's tears, spilling freely down his chest.

"Oh, Michael!" Her voice, muffled against his skin, was thick with tears. Her fingers dug into him as if clawing for support. "I miss him so much!"

For one miserable moment, drowning in his whirlpool of desire, he could hardly understand what she was talking about. He wanted, with an unforgivable selfishness, to make her stop talking, stop crying. For that short, shameful moment he didn't care what she needed. She had to keep touching him, to keep pouring those liquid-gold sensations over his parched body. He couldn't bear the thought of stopping now.

But, even in the middle of that thought, he knew he had to stop. The intensity of her anguish spoke to something buried deep in him, and even the selfish brute he had become couldn't refuse to respond to it.

"Having you here has brought it all back again." She was sobbing openly. "Oh, God, I miss him so much!"

"I know, Jennie," he said, trying to focus on providing some small comfort to her, wrapping his arms around her trembling body. He mustn't think about how his hopes were floating away. He mustn't think about the possibility that he had just lost his last chance to become a whole man again.

"I really need him, Michael. I need a big brother right now." She swiveled, resting her wet cheek against the muscles of his chest. Her hands kneaded his upper arm, opening and closing in an unconscious rhythm that maddened his blood even while he tried to calm it.

"I know Quinn wasn't always wise," she said. She tried to laugh, but it sputtered and sounded more like a choked coughing. "He was spoiled—we all are, I know that. All he wanted out of life was the fun." She made fists of her hands and pressed them fiercely against Michael's chest. "But he was my brother, my only brother, and, oh, Michael, I loved him so much.''

Michael felt the tightness of unshed tears strangling his throat, and he bent his head to Jennie's moon-silvered hair. "I know, darlin'," he managed to say. "I know." He kissed the crown of her head. "I loved him, too."

He half expected her to challenge that, to rear back and slap him for daring to profess love for the man he had killed. But, amazingly, she didn't. With a helpless mew of sorrow, she subsided against his chest, as if comforted by his simple words.

Her tears fell, silent and hot, for a long time. He stroked her back and whispered wordless murmurs into her hair, and gradually the flow ebbed. The shaking of her shoulders subsided, and her ragged breathing grew relaxed and even.

And finally, when her fist drooped open and drifted softly down to rest, palm up and vulnerable, against his arm, he knew that Jennie slept.

He stood slowly, easing her head onto one of the plump pillows piled up on the sofa. Then he gently tugged her gown over her legs and covered her with the afghan that had been folded across the sofa. She looked so young, so peaceful in spite of the tears that glistened on her cheeks and eyelashes, and he stood there for several minutes, watching her sleep.

And then, with his own tears still burning a hole in his constricted throat, he headed upstairs, to the lonely room that had once belonged to Quinton Kearney.

SOMEBODY NEEDED to turn down the sun. Jennie squinted miserably as she tiptoed out to her car at seven the next morning, walking quietly so that she wouldn't wake her father or aggravate the throbbing that threatened to split her head in two.

As soon as she'd awakened—and sorted through her jumbled thoughts to figure out why she'd been sleeping on the den sofa—she'd decided to leave the house early. Her stomach rebelled at the mere thought of the heavy patio breakfast, and her pride wasn't about to risk seeing Michael this morning.

Not after last night. Her recollection was hazy at best, but even hazy memories were too uncomfortable to dwell on. Had she really cried on Michael's shoulder like a baby? She groaned as softly as she could. Yes, she had. That part was painfully clear.

Why would she do such a thing, especially after Clare had planted such poisonous doubts about Michael's role in Quinn's death? Because she simply hadn't believed Clare, that was why. Clare was a melodramatic person even during the best of times, given to exaggerations and embellishments. Now that she was pregnant and obviously going through a very bad spell with Alex, she was having some pretty ludicrous ideas.

Jennie hadn't expressed her skepticism in terms quite so direct to Clare, but her sister had known how she felt anyway. Predicting dire consequences if Jennie let her "crush" on Michael interfere with her judgment, Clare had stormed into the cottage. For the rest of the afternoon she'd been withdrawn and uncommunicative.

A crush. Had Clare been right, at least about that? Had Jennie never quite recovered from her teenage crush on the glamorous Michael? She had been furious with him, had blamed him, cursed him, hated him—but she wondered now whether she could have kept her anger intact if Michael had stayed in Texas. It was easier to despise him long distance. When he was here, the crush seemed to take over, making her do juvenile things—like cry on his shoulder.

Oh, God, what a complicated mess! As she reached her car, the sun glinted off the hood so intensely it felt like shards of glass hitting her eyes. Placing one hand like a shade over her brow, she fumbled to get her key in the lock.

"Going in early?"

She wheeled around, and then regretted it as the rapid motion made her head swirl and pulse nauseatingly. Putting one hand on the door to steady herself, she glowered at Michael, who was making an annoying habit of appearing out of nowhere.

"Yes, I am," she said, embarrassingly aware that her posture had the unnaturally stiff look of a haughty drunk. Her voice, as best she could tell, had the same quality.

"Well, what a coincidence," he answered with a small smile that made her want to slap him. Or perhaps it was the memory of last night, or the remnants of scotch—whatever it was, the impulse was quite strong. "I'm going in, too."

She noticed then that he was in his business clothes, which fit him like a second skin. Last night, she remembered suddenly, he had been wearing little more than his own skin—her gaze dropped against her will to the spot where the curving scar had been. But this morning it was covered by the snowy white cotton of his exquisitely tailored shirt.

"That's nice," she said. "Would you like a ride?"

His smile broadened in open acknowledgment of her dig. "No," he said, chuckling. "I think I'd better have my own transportation today. No telling where I might have to go on the spur of the moment."

He couldn't have put it more plainly than that. Far from having been swayed by their strange moments of intimacy in the den last night, he was as determined as ever to carry out his mission. She stared at him for a long minute, trying to subdue the crazy swell of disappointment that rolled over her like an incoming wave. Her tears hadn't meant much to him, had they?

She pulled in a deep breath and, opening the car door, tossed her purse inside. It didn't matter. He didn't matter.

The only thing that mattered was Clare, and Jennie already had a plan for getting to see her, if not today then at least tomorrow, provided Brad was willing to cooperate.

In the meantime, if Michael wanted to spend his day trotting around after her, that was fine, too. She had lots of boring errands to do, from one end of the hot town to the other.

"Well, I guess I'll see you later, then," she said as gaily as her pounding headache would allow. She slid into the driver's seat and poked her head out. "Oh, and you might want to be sure you have a full tank of gas. It's going to be a long day."

"I always do," he called pleasantly. When she looked in her mirror, she saw that the damn man was laughing.

BY NIGHTFALL, as he sat in Antonio's Italian Restaurant two booths over from Jennie and Brad, Michael was in a foul humor. Another frustrating day—God, he had forgotten how much patience a tailing job required, even an open one like this.

He had decided last night that the only way to bring this job to a swift close was to make Jennie see that she would never be able to shake him. He knew his Jennie. She wasn't stubborn and headstrong like her siblings. She was practical, and though she might be angry, she would soon accept that the best way to help her sister was to tell Michael where Clare was and why she was running. Or perhaps she would decide instead to confide in her father. Either way, Michael's job here would be over.

But she'd certainly led him a pretty dance today. He had followed her to the dry cleaner, the pharmacy, the shoe store, the boutique and the beauty salon, and he'd been sitting here for two hours, drinking coffee he didn't want while she laughed at every one of Brad's comments. The laughter had to be for Michael's benefit. Brad's sappy Shakespear-

ean quotes couldn't possibly be that funny. Hell, all the co-
medians in the world put together weren't that funny.

She looked fantastic, of course. As well she should, having spent all day dolling herself up for this date. Frankly,
Michael wouldn't have thought that Brad McIntosh, though
obviously a decent enough guy, rated this kind of fire-
power. Brad had seemed a little stunned, too. In fact, his
eyes had practically popped out of his head when Jennie
walked in.

Not that Michael was completely immune himself. But
he'd had the advantage of watching the transformation in
more comfortable increments. When Jennie had finally
come out of the boutique she'd been wearing this new
dress—which was short, tight, lacy and exactly the same
blue as her eyes. It probably cost a fortune, but when he
looked at her in it he didn't even see the dress. All he noticed were two legs that went on forever and two eyes that
sparkled like blue diamonds.

Then the beauty salon. She'd been in there for hours, and
he'd been expecting the result to be some extravagantly ba-
roque creation. Instead, the stylist had smoothed Jennie's
hair into a knotted rope of golden silk lying on the nape of
her neck. Michael had been staring at the knot all through
this endless dinner, wondering exactly where you'd start
pulling to untie it.

"More coffee, sir?" The waiter was too well-trained to
show his annoyance, but clearly he thought Michael had
outstayed his welcome. This wasn't the first time Michael
had regretted giving up drinking. Sobriety was never very
popular with waiters.

"Just your bill, then, sir?" The waiter was obviously
ready to turn this table over to more lucrative customers,
and Michael wondered if he'd have to order a drink to get
the man to go away.

Thankfully, though, the poetry fest was showing signs of breaking up. Jennie was bending, looking for her purse, and Brad was frowning over the check. English majors were rarely good with percentages, Michael thought grumpily, and then wished he hadn't. Not only was it petty and untrue—also it was transparently the comment of a very jealous man. And why on earth should he be jealous? Jennie wasn't his. Never had been, never would be. It was absurd to let a shared bowl of popcorn and a tight blue dress give him Neanderthal ideas about untying that silky knot and using it to drag her off to his cave.

He tossed back the bitter dregs of cold coffee. God—listen to him! He had to get out of this town. Fast. Look at the state he had been in last night! He'd been ready to tear Jennie's virginal nightgown to shreds, ready to throw her on the floor and make love to her until neither one of them could move for a week. So what if it violated the trust Arthur had put in him? So what if Jennie hated him, though she'd been too tipsy to remember it? Michael hadn't cared about any of that. He had *wanted,* more like a beast than a man, and he'd been fully prepared to simply snatch what he wanted.

He couldn't quite say, even now, what had stopped him. He only knew that he couldn't be sure he would stop next time, if she were fool enough to let there *be* a next time. Sooner or later the beast would be stronger than the man and— Well, he had enough haunting his dreams without adding that.

But he might have spoken a moment too soon. Jennie and Brad were strolling toward the restaurant's front door, and the professor had his arm around Jennie's bare shoulders amiably. It wasn't a sexual embrace, nothing too tight, no stroking or squeezing. Even so, the sight awakened the beast.

"Parting is such sweet sorrow," Michael heard Brad saying, and Michael nearly choked on his last swallow of coffee.

Oh, perfect, Michael thought. What else? But Jennie was laughing, and at that moment, Michael could quite sweetly have parted Professor Romeo from a couple of his front teeth.

Instead, proud of his restraint, Michael tossed down the fifty percent tip that always managed to turn irritable waiters into his best friends and followed the pair out to the parking lot without touching a hair on Brad's very hairy head. Score one more for the good guys—so far it was gentleman, two; beast, nothing. But he could tell by the tension that coiled through his body that the beast hadn't left the field yet.

Brad departed in his car, going west, so it was just Michael and Jennie, one car behind the other like a mini parade, as they headed east toward the Triple K. And they clearly were headed straight home. Clare would have to do without seeing her little sister tonight, Michael thought with just a tiny twinge of guilt. As Brad might have quoted, sometimes you have to be cruel only to be kind. By tomorrow Jennie should be ready to talk.

They were halfway to the ranch when his car phone rang. It was Lisa, and even through the static he could tell from her breathless hi that she had news.

"I'm not sure how it fits in," she said, getting right to the point, "but it's important. It's from Clare's doctor."

"What? Is she sick?"

"Oh, maybe a little," Lisa said, chuckling. "In the mornings, mostly, I'd wager. You see, the beautiful Clare, absentee wife of Alex Todd, is going to have a baby."

THEY PULLED into the Triple K's circular driveway at nearly
the same moment, so, with a great show of courtesy, Jennie
waited patiently for Michael to join her at the front steps.

"What a coincidence that you decided to eat at Antonio's tonight, too," she trilled. Though she'd had only half
glass of wine, she was feeling a little frisky. Michael might
have penned her in all day today, but Brad had agreed to
help her carry out the perfect scheme for meeting Clare tomorrow night.

Pleased with the scheme and with herself, she adjusted the
draped shoulders of her new dress and smiled brightly. "You
really should have joined us."

Michael's answering smile was equally phony. "I would
have, but I thought I heard Brad say something about a jug
of wine, a loaf of bread, and thou." He shrugged and
cocked one amused eyebrow. "I'm pretty sure he didn't say
anything about thou and thy private detective."

"No," she said, suddenly more subdued, stung by his
comfortable admission that he would have felt a third wheel
at their table. The idea of Brad as her boyfriend didn't seem
to ruffle a single one of his feathers.

She swallowed a lump of dashed pride. Had she really
been hoping to make him jealous? Well, if so, that had been
a particularly foolish hope. She looked at him now, loung-
ing against the wrought-iron railing, moonlight creating a
milky aura around his dark, wavy hair. No, a man like Michael wouldn't consider Brad a real rival.

And for what? For little Jennie, whom he still thought of
as a child? Maybe he was right. Only a child could have
imagined Michael Winters being jealous of Brad McIntosh.

Suddenly all the pleasure seemed to drain out of the night.
The sequins scattered across her dress winked at her, mock-
ing her vanity. She had felt so beautiful when she put it on.
She knew it left no doubt that she was no longer a girl—this

was a woman's dress, molded over a woman's body. Some dumb remnant of wounded pride had wanted desperately for him to notice that.

But he didn't care any more tonight than he had six years ago. She was just Quinn's kid sister. She couldn't have gotten him to notice this ridiculously overpriced dress unless she'd had Clare's address painted on it.

"No," she said again. "I guess not. Well, good night. I think I'll sit on the patio for a minute before I come up."

"What?" He frowned playfully. "No late, late show?"

She flushed. He *would* remind her of that. She wondered edgily how much of what she remembered was accurate, how much was the result of whiskey and wishful thinking. She had thought, for instance, that just for a moment, she had seen a hot desire in his eyes. When he had put her hand on his side, showing her his scar... Or had it been merely the reflection of her desire in the dark depths of his eyes?

Well, whatever it had been, she'd pretty effectively blown it, hadn't she? Touching him had sent her into some sort of emotional overload, and the next thing she knew she'd been sobbing like a wet rag doll in his arms. Hardly the most sophisticated move in the world. There was something about a red, drizzling nose that drove thoughts of wild sex right out of men's heads.

"Not tonight," she said, her embarrassment taking refuge in an oblique sarcasm. "There's nothing worth staying up for."

But he showed no signs of understanding her barbed remark. "Well, good night, then," he said politely, and turned to unlock the front door. The foyer was in shadow, the interior of the house much darker than the moonlit night, so as he entered and shut the door behind him she had the strange sensation that the house simply swallowed him up.

Which left her to go into the back garden alone. Though she no longer had any inclination to sit on the patio, she had announced her intention to do so, and she'd be damned if she'd let him know his absence had spoiled it for her.

With desultory steps she wandered around the side of the house, following the narrow brick path without looking up until she reached the honeysuckle trellis that ran along one edge of the patio. Their scent hung in the air, and she stopped, breathing in the rich sweetness. Sighing, she leaned her shoulder against the trellis, staring out at the silver ripples that sparkled on the black water of the pool.

"Where is she, goddamn it?"

Jennie jumped at the sound of the man's angry voice and grabbed the trellis in both hands as if to use it as a shield. For one shocked moment she thought it was Michael, and her head reeled from trying to reconcile this bitter fury with the lazy good-night he had just tossed her from the doorway.

But then the man stepped out of the patio shadows, and she saw that it wasn't Michael at all. It was Alex Todd.

"Where is she, Jennie?" He was on her in two lunging strides, his glittering eyes boring into hers. He grabbed her shoulders in punishing fingers. She didn't have time to call out.

"Where the hell is my wife?"

CHAPTER SEVEN

AT FIRST pure shock left her speechless, and though with
every passing second Alex's angry fingers dug more deeply
into her upper arms, she couldn't respond. She stared at
him, knowing she looked stupid or stubborn, but unable to
gather her wits.

"Jennifer!" His voice was ragged with tension, and he
shook her slightly. "Answer me!"

She narrowed her eyes, stunned by the uncharacteristic
violence. Although she'd often secretly thought her sister's
husband was, at heart, a weakling, she hadn't ever figured
that he was a brute. Suddenly her sense of outrage over-
came the shocked paralysis. No one, not even her thundering father, had ever treated her so roughly. How *dare* Alex
Todd manhandle her?

"Let go of me," she ordered, trying to wrench her shoulders free. "How long have you been hiding here on the
porch?" She wriggled harder. "I said let *go*, Alex."

But his grip was too tight, and she couldn't free herself.
He shoved his face closer, until his features were distorted.

"Tell me, Jennifer, or I swear you'll be sorry."

Jennie's eyes widened, blood racing through her veins.
Looking across the black shadows of the deserted backyard, which rolled silently into acres of equally deserted
pastureland, she swallowed hard and tried to control the
anxiety that skittered up her spine like tiny, horrid feet.

She thought of her sick father, asleep inside, and of the
timid nurse who dozed in the chair beside his bed. Not much

help there. What about Michael? Quinn's room was on the other side of the house. If she screamed, would he hear her?

Suddenly Clare's suspicions, which had seemed so absurd in the sunny light of noon, came back to haunt her. Michael and Alex, partners in treachery?

A bird launched itself from the branches of a pine, splitting the darkness with its screeching cry, and Jennie's heart froze in her breast. If Clare was right about the two men, then even if Michael heard her... would he come?

"Alex." With effort she kept her voice calm. She couldn't count on anyone riding to her rescue. "You're hurting me."

"No, *you're* hurting *me*." Alex's breath, so close to her face, smelled foul. "You're keeping my wife away from me."

"No, Alex," she said evenly, relieved that the trembling of her nerves didn't vibrate in her voice. Instinctively she knew that, like an angry beast, Alex needed soothing. One false note from her could push him out of control. "You know that's not true. I would never tell Clare how to handle her life. And I couldn't even if I tried. You know that."

"Oh, don't play so damned innocent." In spite of her efforts, Alex's anger was escalating dangerously. His grip was tightening to a grinding pain, bringing tears to her eyes, and Jennie knew she couldn't keep the calm charade up much longer. The truth was that she was just plain scared.

"Alex, please." She hated to beg, but her knees were weak from fear and pain. She wondered whether, caught up in his unthinking fury, he might break her arm. "Please don't— "

"Let go of her, Todd!"

The hard voice came from the French doors, which had opened without a whisper. Alex released Jennie as if he'd been scalded and wheeled toward the house. Clutching her aching arms, Jennie sagged against the trellis as relief washed over her. It was Michael. Thank God, it was Michael.

"What the hell do you think you're doing, Alex?" Michael stepped out onto the patio, his form magnified by the shadows. Suddenly Alex, whose dandified elegance made him look almost effeminate next to Michael, seemed diminished.

"I'm trying to make Jennie tell me where my wife is, that's what," Alex said with a fairly good show of indignation, but his voice had lost its desperate edge.

With bitter pleasure, Jennie noticed Alex didn't risk approaching Michael physically. In fact, the smaller man had taken a couple of unobtrusive steps backward, away from the looming shadow in the doorway.

"Not that it's any of *your* business," Alex finished angrily, lifting his chin to adjust his tie.

"I think it is." With deliberate steps, Michael crossed the patio, his face coming slowly into the moonlight. It was a strange, frightening face, rugged with sharp angles and deep hollows that filled with shadows. Under his lowered brows, his dark brown eyes were pools of liquid black.

"Hey, listen," Alex began, but he didn't get to finish the sentence. Michael had planted himself between Alex and Jennie, and his stance was intimidating, though he didn't lift a single threatening finger.

"Don't *ever*," Michael said with quiet menace, "touch her again."

Alex looked confused, and he smoothed his thin blond mustache nervously. "Well, hey," he sputtered, waving a hand toward Jennie. "I wasn't going to hurt her or anything."

"That's right," Michael agreed with that same underrated power. "And you aren't ever going to, not while I'm here."

"Hell, Michael," Alex protested, and Jennie could see beads of sweat standing on his forehead. "I thought the old man hired you to help find Clare. I didn't know you were getting paid to bodyguard baby sister, too."

"I'm not," Michael said. "I'm throwing that in for free."

"Yeah? Ah..." Alex flicked a quick, assessing glance from Michael to Jennie and back again. A tentative smile quirked one corner of his lips. "Oh, I get it. Decided you can catch more flies with honey, right?"

For a moment Michael didn't answer. His right arm jerked slightly, but the movement was so small Jennie wondered if she'd imagined it.

"Right," he said finally, his tone clipped. "Something like that. Now why don't you go on back to New York, Alex, and leave the investigating to me?"

"Well, I don't know," Alex said, and it was clear that he was too upset to be put off so easily. "Clare's been gone for over two weeks. Are you getting anywhere or not?"

Michael moved forward. "Why don't we talk about that later?" he asked smoothly, putting his hand on Alex's back and pushing lightly. "Come on. I'll walk you to your car."

Alex bestowed one last resentful glance on Jennie, but he didn't make any more threats. Instead he turned away with a pointed silence and let Michael guide him toward the brick path.

A heavy feeling dragged at Jennie's heart as she watched them. *Later.* She knew what Michael meant. Later, when Jennie wasn't around to hear them.

Tears suddenly filled her eyes. Oh, God, she wasn't up to all this. She couldn't fight them both. Her arms hurt where Alex had bruised them, and she was so tired she didn't think she could stand up one moment longer.

Painful emotions had been flashing through her ever since Michael had arrived at the Triple K, like electricity through a conduit. But the messages were confusing and contradic ory, sparking and coursing and then doubling back on one nother.

Just minutes ago, when Michael had first come onto the atio, she'd felt a surge of gratitude so powerful that she'd hought it might physically sweep her into his arms. But ow, as he walked away with Alex, murmuring quietly, naking plans that he clearly didn't want her to hear, a fiery isillusionment streaked through her, following nerve paths hat led directly to her heart.

Except... She rubbed her forehead, trying to pinpoint the law in the logic. Except that Michael hadn't sounded phony when he'd found Alex shaking her. He'd sounded furious.

Her doubts lifted one millimeter as she remembered that one. Wasn't it possible that he was just humoring Alex, aying whatever it took to get him out of here? Maybe. But ow could she ever be sure? She dropped her head against the trellis and shut her eyes. Nothing was clear, except her intense desire to believe that Michael had been shocked by Alex's behavior, and that he would never condone anything that would hurt her or Clare. She breathed deeply. *Or* *Quinn.*

Tears seeped under her closed lids, moistening her eyelashes. Oh, she was so tired, so numb, as if her system had sorted out under the strain.

"Jennie, are you all right?" In what seemed like only a moment, Michael was at her side again, close enough that the scent of him mingled with the honeysuckle. Distantly she heard the rev of an engine and the scattering of pebbles as a car drove away.

"It's okay," Michael said softly. "He's gone."

She didn't answer. She couldn't speak—she couldn't even think anymore.

"Jennie?" His voice was soft, so soft it might have been the whisper of the wind. But it reached deep inside her, and she realized with dismay that she wasn't completely numb

after all. New, strange flashes sparked through her veins
responding to the gentling tones that were so unconsciously
seductive.

She forced herself to turn away, afraid to start the whole
painful process over again, but he caught her by the upper
arm and held her. When his hand touched the bruises Alex
had left behind she winced, and a small, involuntary cry got
halfway through her throat before she could trap it there.

"What is it?" Michael's fingers slid quickly down to her
elbow, away from the tender spot, and he tugged at her,
pulling her into the one clear patch of moonlight. Lifting her
arm, he rotated it slightly, exposing the purpling skin.

"Damn him," he said, low and rough. "He hurt you."

"No," she lied, but the sound was choked. Michael was
exploring her other arm, frowning at the bruises that already stood out in four dark ovals, the imprint of angry
fingertips. He touched that arm, too, and his feather-light
strokes made it hard for her to breathe, let alone speak.

"Jennie," he said harshly, his breath like hot summer air
on her bare skin. "I'm so sorry, sweetheart."

"It's all right." She tried to ignore the shivers that rose
under his touch, shivers that spilled from her arms into her
breast and then into some deep cavern inside her, filling her
with a shimmering light. "I'm fine."

But she was lying. She wasn't fine. She was melting. She
told herself to go inside, to stop this dangerous intimacy
before it went any further, but her limbs wouldn't obey.

And then he moved two small steps toward her, his body
so close he blocked the moonlight, cloaking them both in
shadows.

"Jennie," he murmured. The word was a question, and
she knew that the answer he sought was merely her silence,
her mute acknowledgment that she wanted to stay, wanted
him to stand here, a breath away.

When she didn't speak, he said it again. "Jennie." But this time it was not an asking. It was a promise.

Slowly, winding his hands in hers, he lifted her arms up, bringing them just over her head to rest against the trellis behind her, where the pursed lips of the honeysuckle pressed, velvet sweet, against her wrists.

She didn't resist, though she felt strangely vulnerable, as if by locking her hands in the gentle prison of his fingers he somehow opened the most private places of her soul.

He didn't press his advantage. He merely held her there, and she felt a building tension, a mindless heat, fill the aching space that lay between them. A shiver of anticipation ran jaggedly through her as she waited for... for anything. For whatever he wanted to happen.

Finally he moved. Bending his head, he touched his lips to the sensitive skin inside her left arm, drifting a warm kiss like a balm over the bruises. She made a sound somewhere between a sigh and a moan, and without lifting his head to look at her, he moved to the other arm, ministering to it with the same trailing softness. Surely, she thought, falling slowly into a bottomless well of sensation, the marks would vanish under that kiss.

His lips were tender, but in no way tentative. He was sure of his warm magic, and he kept moving with a slow, sensual cadence, from one arm to the other, as if he were weaving a sparkling net between them. She could almost feel the soft, glittering threads, like some enchanted bondage, tying her arms to the trellis, to each other, to his lips...

He never touched anything but her arms, never let his lips fall once, even once, on her throat, her shoulders, her breast, her cheeks, until those places began to tingle with need, and she asked with an inarticulate murmur for things she couldn't quite put words to.

As if he understood, his fingers tightened on hers, crushing honeysuckle between their palms, releasing a quiver of perfume. With one strong, sure movement, he pulled her slowly to him, placing her trembling hands on either side of his head. And then, abruptly, he released her.

Bereft, she pulled in a quick gasp, and deprived of his touch, instinctively her fingers burrowed into the dense silk of his hair. They found the warm pulse just behind his temple, cupped the full hardness of his crown. With another small cry, this one of open need, she pulled his head to hers.

"Michael," she said, just as he had moments ago spoken her name, in a litany of confusion and desire. And then their lips met in the honeyed darkness with a blind, unerring recognition.

It was like coming home. Oh, she knew his mouth, knew it as if from some memory that had never existed. She knew that it would be confident and firm—and yet wondrously pliable and seductive, the hard, masculine ridges of his lips molding to her softer warmth with a practiced ease. She knew it would be sweet, musky and minty all at once, and it was, oh, God, it was.

Michael's kiss. She had wanted this for so long. Even while she had hated him with every beat of her heart, in some deeper part of her, where the tiny, fiery fragments of her soul burned low and out of sight, she had wanted it. She tightened herself against him, asking for more.

With a low groan that vibrated against her lips, he answered quickly, tensing from shoulder to thigh. Keeping one hand behind her head, he let the other fall to her lower back, and then with both palms he pressed her to him. With a shocked thrill, she felt the rigid thrust of his arousal, and at the same instant he nudged her lips apart, flicking his tongue against the moist and tingling darkness.

The two sensations shot through her like flaming arrows, one rising through her midsection, the other driving down to meet it, and for a dizzied moment she thought she might faint.

But she didn't. Instead, she was jolted into a new level of awareness, where every sense, every nerve was alive and humming with desire. She couldn't get close enough, couldn't take his kiss deep enough, couldn't touch enough of him.

"Michael," she moaned again, unconsciously moving her hips, dragging sequins over wool, as she tried to find the connection that would finally satisfy this tormenting urgency. "Oh, Michael, I don't think I can bear it."

As if puzzled, he pulled his head away slowly, and with glittering eyes that seemed to have absorbed the moonlight, he searched her face.

"Why?" he asked softly, and his voice was distorted, thick and deep and somehow swollen, like his lips.

She touched those lips with two shaking fingers. "I don't know," she whispered, and her voice was trembling, too. "It feels too—" She tried to laugh, suddenly ashamed of her obvious naïveté. Why had she spoken at all? She might have broken the spell. "Too wonderful."

One side of his mouth rose, and the brief white flash of his smile glinted in the muted light. "Too wonderful?" His hand slid down across the curve of her bottom. "I would have said it was perfect."

Reflexively she arched to meet that caress, like a kitten asking for affection, and the motion tilted her pelvis toward his. As their bodies connected, he sucked in air sharply, and his fingers tightened on her soft skin.

"Jennie," he said, his voice strangled and foreign. He exerted a slight pressure on her hips, nudging her a safe couple of inches from him. "We need to talk first."

Talk? Staring at him, stunned, she cursed her own stupidity. She should have known better than to speak, better than to try to put clumsy, stolid words to this vaporous magic. She didn't want to talk. She didn't want to remember that he was supposed to be her enemy. And she didn't want him to remember that she was little Jennie, who had always sought his advice and counsel as if he were another big brother. Her heart knocked at her ribs. She thought she would die if he suddenly pulled back and turned big-brotherly on her now.

She wouldn't let that happen. He wanted her, and she would make him admit it. Molding her hips to his, she shifted subtly against him. "What about this?" she asked, trying to sound sexy and sophisticated. "Maybe we should talk later."

Even as she spoke, she blushed, and she could only hope the moonlight would drain the self-conscious color from her burning cheeks. She suddenly wondered whether her attempt at being slightly wanton had sounded merely trashy. There was such a fine line between being seductive and being vulgar.

"Jennie," he said, his voice low and firm. "Look at me."

She couldn't bring herself to obey. Humiliation was already stinging her eyes. Of course he was disgusted—he probably found this display as unappealing as her tears last night. Oh, God, what had gotten into her?

Finally he tucked his knuckle under her chin and lifted her face. "Honey, I'm really not quite an animal," he said, a wry smile softening his voice. "I can wait for that."

Could he? How? She took a deep breath and met his eyes. "But I don't think I can," she said, the sentence requiring more courage than she had thought she possessed. And more honesty than was wise, probably. But the throbbing inside her was torturous, like a cruel fist milking the confession from her racked body.

"I want you, Michael," she said, and her voice held an aching, desperate note. "I always have. I can't help myself."

It almost sent him over the edge. She could feel it in the slight tremor that rippled through him, in the hard fingers that gripped the swell of her hips, and she could hear it in the rasp of his breath. But he fought the reaction, and somehow she was sure that he would win. Oh, he was too strong.

"I know, sweetheart." He looked at her, all silver and gray in the moonlight, and unbearably handsome. "But you'll hate me in the morning—and you'll hate yourself, too, if we don't talk first. There are too many things we haven't sorted out yet."

Reading the resolution in his face, she swallowed and tried to find her balance. She wouldn't beg. "You mean Clare?"

He nodded. "And Alex. He got pretty rough with you tonight." He touched her bruised arms lightly, but Jennie didn't really notice any discomfort. Her overstrung nerves could only register that her body was no longer close enough to his. It was as if she could feel him slipping away. A sob ballooned painfully at the base of her throat.

"Is that why Clare ran away from him?" Michael's brows were pulled down in a frown. "Did he abuse her?"

Jennie tried to concentrate, though it was hard to hear her thoughts over the angry clamor of her body.

"No, I don't think so," she said in a monotone as hope drained away. Didn't he see what he was doing? Clare's very name opened up a gulf between them that was unbridgeable. "Clare hasn't said anything about violence."

Michael's frown deepened. "Then maybe this was just because he's overwrought." He stroked her arm, careful not to press the tender places. "It's horrible, but..." His eyes were dark, all the moonlight gone. "If he knows about the baby, then I can almost see why he'd be frantic. His first— his *only* child, taken away from him." He was looking beyond Jennie, into the ghostly pastureland. "Any man would go a little crazy."

"But he doesn't know about the baby," Jennie said numbly. "Clare said she doesn't want him ever to know."

Michael was silent for a long moment. And somewhere in that hollow silence, with a cold flash that seemed to freeze her blood, Jennie realized what she had done. She backed out of his arms, horrified.

Oh, Clare! What kind of ally was she, spilling the most intimate secrets freely? Until she had so stupidly confirmed it, surely Michael had been only guessing about the baby.

"How did you know Clare was pregnant?" Her brittle voice sounded strange to her. She had, in those few glorious minutes spent in his arms, grown used to hearing passion in it.

But Michael didn't seem to hear the transformation, or even to notice that she had moved out of reach. "Alex probably thinks he'll never see either one of them again," he said, as if to himself. He rubbed his hand roughly over his mouth. "My God, he must be mad with it."

"He doesn't know!" She felt a little maddened herself, with anger and with guilt. It was dawning on her why he had been so affectionate when he had rejoined her after dispatching Alex. She had let herself believe that his offer of comfort had flamed into desire in spite of his gallant intentions. Now she saw how absurdly virginal that evaluation was.

Michael hadn't been caught up in a sudden squall of passion. Looking at him now, at his perfectly toned, blatantly masculine body, and at the passionate beauty of his rugged face, she wondered how she could ever have thought so. This would hardly have been Michael's first encounter in the moonlight. He knew exactly where to touch a woman to make her melt, precisely where a rain of kisses would most quickly erode self-control. Oh, he knew everything, and he had used that knowledge, like Pentothal sodium, to coax the truth from the lips he kissed.

Damn him! She could almost taste the bitter drug in her mouth. She had to swallow convulsively. "How did you know?'' she cried hoarsely, not bothering to keep her voice low.

Michael was looking at her blankly, as if her cry had recalled him from some black place far, far away. ''Know that she's pregnant? Her doctor. I've had a man looking into things up in New York. My secretary called tonight with the report.''

''My, you certainly are efficient.'' She ripped off one pale honeysuckle bloom and tore it apart in her hands. ''All your little minions running around the country doing your bidding. And you with nothing to do but mosey on down to Texas and soften the baby sister up with a few well-timed kisses. This is where I'm supposed to swoon, I guess, and pour my little heart out, telling you everything.''

His eyes narrowed, flicking from her tight and angry face to the mutilated blossom and then back again. ''That would be nice,'' he said, his careless tone at odds with his tense body, which he held ramrod stiff. ''But something tells me you're not going to.''

''You're damn right I'm not,'' she said, making a fist around the honeysuckle, though the sticky sap oozed between her fingers and the sweet smell was sickening. ''So you've wasted your time, haven't you? And all those delightful kisses, too. I told you it wouldn't work.''

He was ominously still. ''You can't believe that.''

''But I do,'' she said, low and fierce, staring at the ground. ''I do.''

She could feel his anger. She raised her gaze defiantly and caught her breath at the grim expression she saw there. At first she thought he might grab her, might shake her just as Alex had done. But he didn't move. Fists clenched at his sides, he took two deep breaths that went all the way to his diaphragm. He loosened his fists, ran one hand through his tousled hair, and then, to her surprise, he smiled.

"Well, before you make up your mind completely, let me offer another suggestion." Obviously more relaxed, he strolled around behind her and sat on the edge of the long picnic table, one foot hooked on the attached seat, the other stretched out before him. "What about this scenario? *You* were the one with an ulterior motive here, not me."

"*I* was?" She had to swivel to see him, and when she did he was shrouded in shadows. She was the one left standing in a stream of moonlight, exposed and confused. What was he getting at? "What motive could I possibly have had?"

"Getting me to agree to call off the investigation."

"What?" It was like a slap in the face. Her breath came quickly, hot and indignant. "That's ridiculous!"

"Is it?" He cocked his head, considering. "Actually, I think it makes more sense than your scenario. After all, I don't have any history of despising you, do I? I wasn't the one who was calling names and vowing lifelong hatred just two days ago. Don't you think it's rather suspicious that suddenly you're in my arms, telling me you can't wait to jump into my bed?"

Her hands flew to her face. Her cheeks burned as if the words he had just tossed at her were scalded water. "I— It wasn't like that," she sputtered, but she heard how weak her protest was. He was right, in a way. On the surface, it *had* been like that. It was only deep inside her, where no one could see, that it all made sense. Deep in her heart, where, ever since she first met him, love and longing had always been hiding, waiting for a night like this to burst free.

"Wasn't it?"

"You know it wasn't." She folded her arms across her chest, trying to calm the clumsy, scrambling rhythm of her heart. "I was upset—Alex had frightened me. And this trouble with Clare—well, it's been a terrible strain." She tried to read his face, but the shadows distorted everything.

"And then you were suddenly here, being so kind and gentle, it took me by surprise. And the night was so... The moonlight...."

"Liar." The soft word seemed to float from his lips, and she stopped in mid-sentence, shocked.

"What did you say?"

"I said you're lying, Jennie." Standing suddenly, Michael walked slowly to where she stood. "It wasn't the moonlight, or Alex, or any of a thousand stupid excuses I'm sure you could invent. And it wasn't manipulation—not for either one of us. You damn well know that."

"But you said you thought that I—"

"No." He stopped her words by placing his forefinger gently across her lips. "I just wanted you to see how easy it is to twist this into something ugly."

He smiled as her lips struggled to form a new protest, only to be quieted by the barrier of his finger. "I don't believe for a minute that you were willing to bed me just to keep me from finding Clare. You hadn't given Clare a thought since I first touched you." He slid his finger across the line of her full lower lip, his eyes gleaming in the semidarkness. "And neither had I."

Her lips tingled, as if his finger had left a sparkling afterglow in its path. Could he be right? She was hopelessly muddled, her feelings having raced from one direction to another, then back again, until she'd lost all sense of reason. Which way should she turn now?

"Michael...I'm so confused," she said brokenly, and he cupped her cheek in the warm palm of his hand, as if to brace her. "I don't know what to—"

A tiny metallic peal rang into the night, cutting off her stumbling words. Without moving her head, she glanced at the small telephone that perched on a poolside table between two loungers. The outdoor telephone, the one lazy sunbathers used when they couldn't be bothered to dry off, the one sweaty workmen borrowed when they weren't allowed indoors.

The sound seemed to echo in the night air, and her heart beat in huge, irregular skips. Who could be calling so late?

No second ring followed, but she continued to stare at the telephone. Her father didn't have a telephone in his bedroom—the closest one was in the hall. Not even his nurse could have answered it so quickly. A growing dread slowed her blood.

"What's wrong?" Michael was studying Jennie's face closely. He rubbed her cheek, as if trying to get her attention.

And then, after a silence just long enough for Jennie to be sure it was a second call, the telephone rang again. Again, just once. A cold dread settled in the pit of her stomach, and she finally transferred her wide-eyed, frantic gaze to Michael, who was watching her with a question in his eyes.

One ring, repeated twice. Clare. It was their code for an emergency. Not loneliness, not a request for more groceries, but a real, five-alarm emergency.

Something was dreadfully wrong.

CHAPTER EIGHT

"IT'S CLARE, ISN'T IT?" Michael's hand massaged her cold cheek softly.

She didn't answer, unable to think of a lie that would smooth them past this moment. She had to go to Stewart's Roost immediately. Her arms and legs ached with the need to fly into action. Clare needed her, perhaps desperately. But Michael... Suddenly he seemed like the jailer again, the immovable barrier between her and her sister.

"I have to leave," she said impulsively, the words running together, spoken all at once on a shallow breath.

His hand stilled on her cheek, and he lifted his brows, widening his eyes enough to let the moonlight shimmer against the whiteness that surrounded the deep brown centers.

"Tonight?"

"Yes. It's—" She shook her head, unable to say much without choking. "It could be something serious."

"Then let me go with you." His voice was gentle, and he pressed her icy hand against his chest. Though her fingers were strangely numb, she could sense the steady beat of his heart. "You may need help."

It was tempting. She caught her breath, surprised to discover just how dangerously tempting it was to imagine transferring this exhausting burden to his shoulders. The look in his eyes was tender, as soft as starlight. His hand was warm and strong, quite capable of taking over. And she was so tired.

But she couldn't. With effort she pulled her hand away, for fear the temptation would prove too strong. She had promised Clare—who had predicted bitterly that Michael could wind Jennie around his little finger—that she wouldn't tell him anything.

Later—maybe even later tonight, if everything was all right at the cottage—she would try to explain, to urge Clare to confide in Michael. Until then she had to live with her promise.

"I can't," she said, edging away slightly. She ran her fingers along the prickly surface of the picnic table, pretending to study it. "You know I can't."

Silence. Nervously she looked up, and when she met his eyes, it was as if someone had blown out a candle. Darkness had fallen behind his suddenly blank gaze, a shadow within a shadow.

"I see," he said, staring at her from those black, empty eyes. "You still don't trust me."

"No, it's not that," she said miserably, grabbing the edge of the table, her sequins twinkling with blue fire as she shifted in the moonlight. "It's just that I promised Clare, and she's counting on me—"

"Damn it, Jennie, I don't want to hear all that!" He broke impatiently into her ragged explanation. "Just yes or no. Do you trust me?"

She wanted to say yes. She almost did say it. But as she willed her mouth to form the word, all the old doubts came pouring in like a swarm of locusts, eating away at her courage.

Trust him?

She bowed her head, unwilling to let him read what might be written on her face. She *wanted* to trust him, but should she? What if she had been drugged by his kisses, just as she'd feared? Her desire for this man was so intense it might well have blinded her. Certainly it had stripped her of all the moral indignation and bitterness she had grown so accustomed to over the past six years. Now she felt only a confused vulnerability. She no longer knew what to think—about Clare, about Alex...or even about Quinn and the night he was killed.

But what if, though he denied it so eloquently, blinding her had been Michael's intention all along? Could she really sacrifice Clare's safety just because she had been mesmerized by a pair of brown eyes and the magic of moonlight and honeysuckle?

"Yes or no?"

"I don't know," she stammered, frightened by the raw venom in his voice. "I was trying to explain when—" She cast a wretched glance at the telephone, trying to decide whether dissimulation was worth the effort. It wasn't. He knew perfectly well who had been on the other end of that line. "When Clare called, I was trying to tell you that I just don't know what to think anymore."

"So it's no." Ignoring her smoke screen of verbiage, he spoke acidly, his tone declaring the subject closed. Turning away with a curse, he strode to the edge of the pool where he stood, hands in his pockets, staring into the black, glassy depths. Dancing daggers of moonlight were reflected onto his face, but it was a cold, shifting light, and it made him look odd, more enigmatic than ever.

She turned away, too, bending her head again to the task of plucking a splinter from the table. She didn't argue—from his perspective, he was right. If she didn't know whether she trusted him, then she didn't. Painfully simple logic.

Hearing the soft rustle of his footsteps on the grass, she looked up. He had abandoned his inspection of the pool and was watching her again. He was only a few feet away, and his eyes were narrowed.

"I suppose what I find most curious," he remarked with a strangely remote bitterness, "is that you'd be so damn willing to go to bed with a man you don't trust."

Heat swamped her face. There was no way to deny that, either. He knew she had been his for the taking.

A hundred explanations, a thousand denials, stormed through her thoughts. But none of them was nearly powerful enough to cut through the wall that stood between them. And she was running out of time—it was unforgivably selfish to stand here wishing Michael would understand and forgive her while Clare...

Panic pushed against her throat, and she felt slightly nauseated. She was going to have to come right out and ask for what she wanted.

"Michael," she said, her voice tight with distress, her hands outstretched, placating and pleading. "I have to go."

"Then go," he said harshly. "I can follow you."

"Yes." She blinked and felt two tears streak down her cheeks, tears she hadn't even realized were threatening. "I know that. But I'm asking you not to."

"You're asking me—" With another curse, he slammed his hand onto the table that held the phone, the instrument releasing a tinny ping of protest beneath the violent force of his blow. "You ask one hell of a lot, don't you?"

"I have to," she said, humbled by the knowledge that ultimately everything rested in his hands. His capable hands, once so warm, which now were tensed into fists at his sides.

"What about me?" His voice was more like a growl. "You're not the only one who's made promises, you know. What about my promise to your father?" He looked around the dark property with a wild, barely reined frustration. "And what about what's left of my common sense, which tells me it's not safe, goddamn it, for you to go driving all over creation alone? You don't even know what's wrong, Jennie. You don't know what you could be getting into."

She shrugged helplessly. "I know," she whispered, unable to match his fury. "But I have to ask you to let me go."

For a long time he just stared at her, the heavy rasp of his breathing the only sound in the eerie, silent darkness. Somewhere out in the five thousand acres that were Kearney property, horses and cows chewed the grasses placidly and tired ranch hands were locking up the barns, but right here, right now, Jennie felt that she and Michael were the only two people on earth.

Praying without words, she watched his chest rise and fall for what seemed like a long time. Finally, gradually, a more normal rhythm set in, though his face was still harsh, the lines around his mouth etched deep.

"Don't," he said suddenly. He shut his eyes, as if he was addressing some interior adversary. "Don't do it, Jennie. Don't ask me to go against every one of my instincts."

"I'm sorry," she said, feeling inexplicably like a criminal, acutely aware of the impotence of that perfunctory phrase. She *was* sorry, though for the life of her she couldn't understand why. *He* was the one who was intruding, who was making everything so difficult for Clare and for her. "But I am asking you."

A low rumble of frustration seemed to escape his compressed lips, and squeezing his eyes shut tightly, he tilted his head back. Moonlight poured over his face like a museum spotlight over a marble statue, illuminating every furrow in his brow, every taut muscle in his jaw. How different he had looked a few moments ago, when he had been in her arms. The change was somehow painful, and she wished she had the right to reach out and touch that cold, marbled cheek. She could turn it to warm, responsive flesh again. She knew she could.

But when he brought his head down, the illusion passed. Though he still looked strained, the worst evidence of his difficult decision had been wiped from his features.

His level gaze held only a bitter resignation. "All right, Jennie," he said, his voice flat and tired. "You win."

She felt no triumph—only an incredible wash of relief, and underneath that a tiny sting of sorrow that she would have to leave him now. But she ignored that. The important thing was that she could go safely to Clare.

"Thank you," she said clumsily, clinging to trivial civilities because her own words failed her. "It means a lot—"

"Wait." He interrupted her roughly, putting a hand on her arm to stop her instinctive move toward the driveway. "I want to make one telephone call first."

Immediately suspicion flared, tightening her lungs, cutting off her breath. "To whom?"

But he had already moved toward the telephone and was punching buttons rapidly. With quick steps that set her sequins flashing, she joined him, her nerves skittering. Who was he phoning? Alex? Her palms felt uncomfortably slick, and she rubbed them on her dress. Oh, God, she had forgotten about Alex! Had he agreed to let her go only because he knew that Clare's husband would be following instead?

"Who are you calling?" Her words seemed to echo unnaturally across the silent water beside them. *Please,* she whispered inwardly, *not Alex.*

"An operative." He bit the words out, as if he begrudged her the information. He hooked the telephone between his chin and shoulder and stared into the distance, listening to it ring. "I sent someone after Alex as soon as he left here. I want to be sure they've got an eye on him."

Finally someone answered. She stood there, racked with doubts, not breathing quite properly, while he conducted his terse conversation. She could hear only Michael's end of it, and her mind worked furiously to fill in the blanks.

"Mencken, did you find him? Good. Where is he? Has he checked in yet? Good. Let the in-house man know what you're doing, give him my name and then park yourself outside Todd's room. Keep your cellular phone with you and call me if you hear a peep out of him. I don't care—sit on him if you have to."

She watched numbly as Michael dropped the receiver in its cradle with a clatter. Her doubts were fading, but not completely erased. It had sounded like a genuine conversation, but... was she being too naive? Suppose it was a ruse, something invented to make her think she was safe? She hadn't heard a word spoken at the other end, hadn't even heard the unintelligible rumble that would have proved there was anyone there at all.

She stared at the telephone for a long moment, as if it were a living thing. She knew she was becoming paranoid, and yet the very thought of Alex had paralyzed her. She couldn't tell truth from lie, honesty from charade.

"Go," Michael said curtly. "She needs you."

She looked from him to the phone and to him again. A minute ago her path had seemed to lie straight and clear before her. Now, thinking of leading Alex to Stewart's Roost, where she and Clare would be alone, made her blood run cold.

Observing her blatant indecision, Michael raised one brow and the corner of his mouth followed it up in a sardonic smile that was absolutely devoid of mirth.

"God, this is rich! You don't believe that call, either? You actually think I'm capable of faking it?"

He made a low, disgusted sound and shoved a deck chair out of his way. "Well, I'm sorry, darlin', but frankly I'm just plain sick of trying to convince you that I'm not some diabolical monster. If you want to see Clare tonight, it looks like you'll have to dredge up a little faith in me after all."

CLARE WAS, for once, dry-eyed. Somehow, though, the sight only frightened Jennie more. She had burst through the cottage door in a heated rush, but stopped in her tracks the minute she saw Clare's grim expression.

"Sit down, Jen." Clare gestured weakly toward the seat beside her. "We need to talk."

Slowly Jennie lowered herself onto the edge of the sofa, dropping her keys on the cushion. "Are you okay? Are you hurt?" she asked, but even as she spoke she could tell it wasn't that. Clare was pale, but she was neatly dressed, hair brushed and shining under the light from the nearby lamp.

"No," Clare said in a low-pitched voice, folding and refolding the hands she clasped in her lap. "But I've found out some things that I think you ought to know."

Mutely Jennie nodded, her heartbeat racing as if she had been injected with adrenaline. But she forced herself to sit still. "All right," she murmured.

"Okay." Clare cleared her throat and bit her lip. "God— it's hard to know where to begin. Well, I guess it really began last month, when I got control of my trust from Mom."

Jennie didn't even bother to nod this time. She knew all about that, of course. On Clare's thirtieth birthday, she gained full control of the money their mother had left in trust for her. Both daughters had trust funds, and they were quite large—bigger than expected, since Quinn's share now belonged to his sisters. But Jennie rarely thought about the money. It would be seven years before she inherited hers outright, and she was quite content to wait. She had everything she needed, the interest income and her salary from Kearneyco combining to make her independent. Only her father's ill health had kept her at home.

"It all started then," Clare said, echoing herself with a quiet, distant sound. She sounded almost calm, although Jennie could see that her knuckles were white and bloodless. "I knew Alex had money problems. The restaurants weren't doing all that well, and he's always spent a lot. I fact, he's always run through everything we had, and then some."

Clare twisted her plain gold band around her ring finger, and Jennie noticed that her sister wasn't wearing her large engagement solitaire. Had she ever had it on, here at Stewart's Roost, or had she left it in New York? Jennie couldn't remember.

"Anyway, I didn't realize how bad the problems were until the trust was released," Clare went on. "But then Alex told me the truth. He needed my money—all of it."

"*All* of it?" Jennie's mouth was dry, and the resulting squeak would have been comical if they hadn't been talking about so much money. More than a million dollars. She tried to swallow and found that she couldn't. "*All* of it?"

Clare nodded. "Some of it we'd already borrowed against, so that had to go to the bank right away. And some of it he owed, you know, to the normal places. Restaurants are very expensive to run. But the rest of it he owed to—" She stopped, and for the first time Jennie saw the glimmer of tears shimmering in her eyes. "To people. You know what I mean? Horrible people."

Jennie shook her head, bewildered. "No," she said, struggling to comprehend it. "No, I don't know. This is crazy. Are you telling me Alex had borrowed money from—" It seemed ridiculous even to say the word. They weren't bit players in a second-rate mob film. They were just the Kearney sisters, nice, normal people. "From *gangsters?*"

Clare laughed brokenly, and Jennie thought she heard a hint of hysteria behind the sound.

"No. I don't know. Not exactly." Clare worried nervously at her upper lip. "Alex just said he'd borrowed money to start the restaurants from some people he didn't trust anymore. He said they were getting ugly, and he absolutely had to pay them off right away."

"So what did you tell him? Did you give him the money?"

Clare shook her head. "No. I was angry. I had just found out I was pregnant." She pulled her clasped hands up to rest against her stomach, the gesture apparently unconscious. "I was furious to think he would lose our child's inheritance. Our baby—" She broke off again, looking at her hands. "I wasn't nice about it, Jen."

Jennie could imagine. She felt a little weak just picturing how withering Clare's wrath could be. And yet, hadn't Alex deserved it? A million dollars! Good God.

"We weren't even speaking to each other much." Clare took a deep breath, as if to brace herself to go on. "And then, a couple of days later, while Alex was at work, I got a call. Some man. He told me I'd better give Alex the money."

Clare's lips began to tremble, and she put her fingers over them hastily. The rest of her words were spoken through that muffling barrier. "He had a very nasty voice, insinuating, you know? He had a way of making every word sound like a threat. He said that I might as well just go ahead and hand over the money, because Alex would inherit it all anyway, if anything...if anything happened to me."

For a sickening moment, as the awful meaning of Clare's words sank in, the room seemed to spin. Jennie clutched the scratchy fabric of the couch with both hands, trying to keep from falling off. Her blood roared in her ears, deafening her.

"Oh, Clare," she whispered. "No."

"Yes." Strangely, Clare looked stronger now, as if telling the tale had made it more manageable. "It was clearly a threat. They want my trust money, and they intend to get it one way or another. I guess I panicked. I ran away. I hired an investigator to find out who these people are, and I've been waiting for news ever since." She looked around the room, as if seeing its mottled walls for the first time. "Almost three weeks in this dump. But their identity was buried pretty deep. And now I know why, Jennie, because now I know who they are."

Jennie stared, unwilling to ask. She didn't want to know. Whatever the name was, it carried the power to turn her flighty, fun-loving sister into this quiet, white-faced woman who suddenly seemed at least ten years older and a thousand years wiser. She bit her dry, numb lips, willing Clare to be silent, and held her breath. She didn't want to know.

But Clare refused to spare her. "It's the same men who owned the warehouse where Quinn was killed, Jennie," she said in an appalling monotone. "It's the Mitchell family."

MICHAEL WAITED UP most of the night, fully dressed, staring at the alternating lines of darkness and moonlight that crisscrossed his bedroom walls like prison bars.

In that tense, expectant state, he heard every sound that echoed through the rambling house—the nurse's soft-soled shuffle as she trekked to the bathroom, the fussing of old wood as it settled, the scratching of crickets that occasionally stopped, as if by design, with an expectant hush, and then resumed. He even learned to predict when the air conditioner would kick on with an electric hum.

He shifted restlessly. How could there be so many noises in one silent night—and why were none of them Jennie?

Finally, near dawn, the sound he'd been waiting for came. He heard her car, heard her key twist in the stubborn lock, heard her slow footsteps climbing the stairs.

Jennie. She was home. She was safe.

He sat up in bed, his muscles tensing, staring at his door. He had kept his promise—he had waited here in this tortured limbo of worry and frustration the whole black night long. Now he wanted her to come to him. She owed him that.

He watched her in his mind, willing her to make the turn toward his room, willing her to knock or just to shove open the door, willing her to come to him, to tell him about Clare. Come, Jennie, come...

But she didn't. Her footsteps faded away, and his chest tightened, disbelieving, as he heard her door shut softly. An almost uncontrollable anger, a furious sense of betrayal, pounded in his temples. She wasn't going to come.

He could hardly believe how much it hurt. He forced himself to breathe normally, trying to manage the grinding disappointment, struggling to accept what he should have known all along. She would never forgive him. She would never trust him. Never.

In a sudden burst of fury, he swung his legs over the bed, dragging the bedclothes into disarray, and stood up with a violence that, as his body moved in front of the window, bent the bars of moonlight. The digital clock on the dresser glowed faintly blue, its numbers visible across the room. Four-thirty. She'd been out all night, and she wasn't even planning to give him the courtesy of an explanation.

Over the hours he had grown thickheaded, exhausted if not actually sleepy. His temples ached and his eyes were as gritty as sand. But the angry racing of his blood cleared his head miraculously, and he felt wide awake and ready for battle. Not even a word, not even the human decency to come and let him know she was all right?

In that high-fired indignation, he got as far as the door. And then, with an abrupt clenching of his gut, a sudden icy hardening of his anger, he knew he couldn't go to her. Why should he beg for a crumb of information, a word of reassurance? Damn it, she owed him! He had done something for her tonight that he hadn't done for anyone in six years—he had set aside his judgment and let his heart rule his head. If she didn't appreciate what that had meant to him...

She ought to know he wasn't a lapdog, to be told to sit and stay and heel at her whim. But if she didn't, then, by God, she would soon see how rare such a concession was. Starting right now, he was going to do his job. And, for the first time since he'd set foot on the Triple K, he was going to do it with a vengeance. He was going to find Clare Kearney, even if she was hiding in the caverns of the moon.

Paying no heed to the rumpled state of his clothes, though the creases of his shirt were like a road map of every sleepless toss and turn, he flicked on all the lights, threw open his briefcase and started jabbing the buttons of the telephone. He hoped little Jennie was getting some sleep, because, come morning, there wasn't going to be a secret in Texas that was safe from him.

CHAPTER NINE

JENNIE DIDN'T LEAVE the house until almost six o'clock the next evening, but when she did, Michael was right behind her. Within ten minutes he knew where she was going—to Silver Palms, the subdivision that was home to several hundred doctors and lawyers and, according to Michael's research, one Brad McIntosh.

Michael's lip curled as he realized her destination. So she was going to run to Professor Romeo, eager to tell him—every one of the details that Michael, like a damn fool, had waited all night to hear. He glared at Jennie's red car as it flashed down Silver Palm Drive. It didn't help to know that he would have gladly recited every damn sonnet Shakespeare ever wrote if it could have lured Jennie into his room last night.

But that was last night. Today he was back to being numb. He probed gingerly at his emotions, checking for tender spots. His years of disciplined indifference, sealing his heart away in an airtight place, served him well now. There was a distant throb somewhere, but he couldn't quite feel it. No, he would be okay. Unless he actually reconstructed the feel of her lips on his, he was absolutely fine. That would fade, too, with enough work and a little time.

Twenty-three Silver Palm Drive was not what Michael had expected. The two-story house, which backed onto the waterway, was at the heart of a cul-de-sac that seemed entirely populated by kids playing catch with their dads, while their moms smiled and knelt over flower pots.

Suburban heaven. Michael recognized it immediately. It was the kind of life he and Brooke had tried so futilely to create during their hellish six months of marriage. Well, the accident had put a permanent end to those fantasies. Now he lived in a town house with only an eight-foot square of grass in back. If he wasn't ever going to play catch in the yard, why spend any time mowing it?

But it was Brad's house, all right. There was no mistaking McIntosh's hulking body, or the big bear hug he wrapped around Jennie the minute he saw her. Michael shoved back against the seat, controlling the urge to smash his fist through the window as Brad closed the door behind her.

Michael waited. Gradually the kids went in, and the sun began to drop, washing the houses in a deep red-gold glow. What the hell were Brad and Jennie doing in there, anyway? He had assumed they would at least go out to dinner, but now his mind conjured up uncomfortably vivid images of the two of them in the kitchen, sipping wine, stirring a sizzling pan, laughing playfully as they tasted things off each other's spoons.

Or were they sitting out on a back porch overlooking the water, watching the romantic sunset stain the water crimson?

The water. Michael peered intently at the house, suddenly feeling like a fool. The inlet led directly to the Gulf of Mexico, and from there to the whole blasted world! Good God, it was the perfect escape.

Cursing under his breath, he climbed out of the car. It had been a long time since he'd made such a dumb mistake. As soon as he realized Jennie had entered a waterfront house, he should have called in another operative to watch the back. And yet he'd been sitting here for hours, scowling at the house like a jealous lover spying on his two-timing girlfriend.

Disgusted, he jogged briskly to the corner and cut through to the water. She could have been gone for hours, for all he knew. Damn! Why was it so hard to remember to be a professional when it came to Jennie?

But this was his lucky day. She was on the back deck, her blond hair copper in the dying light, ruffling around her face like a halo. Dressed in a loose-fitting cotton dress sprigged with tiny blue flowers, she was leaning against the railing, as if she was too tired to stand on her own.

She stared, absolutely unmoving, for a long, long time, and Michael wondered what she was seeing. He scanned the horizon, but saw nothing there except a runabout that skimmed by, kicking up a foaming wake that was almost strawberry in the sunset. And, of course, the distant outlines of some spit islands, which surely couldn't have been all that fascinating.

Unless… Unless that's where Clare was. He looked again, his interest quickening. Sand in Jennie's car, the kid at the garage had said. He tried to remember how many islands there were, and whether any had accommodations that would suit Clare.

But he couldn't remember. He hated to take his eyes off Jennie, but he had to go get the map out of his car. He watched her one last moment, allowing himself, with a self-destructive indulgence, to toy with the question of whether she was more beautiful in the molten gold of sunset or in the pale cream of moonlight.

There was no answer. She was always Jennie, and always the most beautiful thing he'd ever seen. His abdomen clenched, as if warding off an invisible blow, and he had to bite down on his lower lip to keep from calling her name.

"Jennie!" But it wasn't his voice. It was Brad's, carrying with infuriating clarity over the water. "Jennie, come back in!"

At the sound, Jennie turned, her hair blowing across her lips like soft fire, and in a second or two Brad appeared on the deck. Smiling, he joined her at the railing, pulling her into his arms with the practiced ease of a friend—or a lover.

Which one was it? "Jennie...." This time it was Michael's voice, low and urgent, like a throbbing in his ears.

But she couldn't hear him. Tucking her arms against her body, her fists under her chin like a frightened child, she rested her head on Brad's chest and let the sunset wrap them in a soft red glow. After a long minute, in which every muscle in Michael's body coiled into a savage mass of pain, Brad kissed the top of her head and gently began to lead her into the house.

"Jennie!" The word came hoarsely, like a groan, from Michael's anguished, angry throat. How dare Brad hold her like that? How dare she let him? Just last night she had been in *his* arms. He remembered exactly how soft she had felt, and how she had smelled of honeysuckle. Now her steps were slow, but Brad's arms were around her shoulders, easing her forward. They were almost out of sight.

"Don't," Michael whispered, impotent to stop them, trying to will her to stop herself. "Damn you, Jennie. Don't."

JENNIE FELT as if she hadn't slept in a week. It was almost four in the morning before she stood up from her cold, stale cup of coffee, rubbed her hands over her tired eyes and began hunting for her purse.

Clare, who had been brought over by Brad much earlier in the day, was half asleep, sitting up against the headboard of the bed in Brad's guest room. She roused herself when she realized Jennie was leaving. "Tomorrow, then?"

Jennie smiled. "Yeah. You get a little sleep. Brad said he'd wake you up about eight and run you back to Stewart's Roost. Just pack as quickly as you can, and I'll be there as soon as I can.''

Clare nodded soberly, and Jennie felt a rush of the new respect she had gained for her sister over this long night of frantic planning. Gone was the princess, the snobbish, moneyed matron who had always slightly annoyed her younger sister. It was the one truly special thing to come out of this whole unhappy nightmare.

During the past few hours, closeted in Brad's spare room, they had talked over their choices. Clare's private detective was still looking for information, but if he didn't find anything very soon, Clare and Jennie both knew something drastic had to be done. Clare couldn't keep running forever.

The subject of divorce came up, of course, but Clare seemed strangely reluctant to commit to that. It wouldn't get processed fast enough to protect her, she insisted. Besides, once the Mitchell brothers caught wind of divorce proceedings, they would move heaven and earth to find Clare before the money slipped out of their grasp for good.

In the end, they had decided it would be safest just to make over the trust to Alex. ''It's only money, Clare,'' Jennie had said firmly. ''It's not worth dying for.'' And Clare had merely nodded.

After she had run away once, though, they couldn't be sure the Mitchell brothers would be content with promises. Neither of them doubted for a moment that Clare was really at risk. They had seen the Mitchell brothers at Quinn's inquest, and the memory of their ruthless faces had never left them. Both brothers had iron-clad alibis for the night of the robbery, but Jennie knew they'd been questioned extensively by the police.

So until the transfer of the trust could be finalized, Clare had to continue to protect herself. They'd decided that Clare would have to move—to another city, at least. Another state would be even better. It had been a terrible self-indulgence for her to hide so close to Jennie. Anyone looking for her would undoubtedly start with the family members. Now that they knew who they were dealing with, such luxuries weren't worth the risk.

"What about Michael?" Clare had begun turning down the linens, neatly folding the spread and setting it on the chest at the foot of the bed. "Are you still planning to get someone to investigate him, too?"

"I have to, Clare. I have to know." Jennie didn't look at her sister, tired of the debate. Clare had argued against it vehemently, saying that Michael wasn't important enough to waste valuable time on right now. But even over Clare's objections, Jennie had decided to hire a second private detective to look into Michael's finances.

"Why? We've already agreed that we can't risk trusting him. We know what Quinn's insurance policy was worth. It wasn't enough to launch Alex's restaurants, and you know it wasn't enough to set up Michael Winters in such splendor, either." Clare was too tired, obviously, to give the discussion her full energies. Three hours ago she had been much more adamant. "Oh, Jennie, why does it matter so much to prove whether he's involved with the Mitchells, too?"

Jennie didn't answer. She wasn't really sure why. She just knew she had to find out. Had his grand success been bought with Mitchell money? With Quinn's blood?

That was clearly what Clare thought, but Jennie was oddly resistant. Was it possible, she asked herself, that her body could have been melting in the arms of a cold-blooded killer? Something deep, deep inside kept crying no. But her common sense—and her sister—reminded her sternly that women all over the world fell in love with bad men every day.

She dropped down on the bed, suddenly short of breath. Love. A tear pearled in the corner of her eye as her heart constricted with misery and confusion. Love? Oh, dear God...

"I may be falling in love with him, Clare," she said abruptly, helplessly, looking through her tears at her sister's horrified face. She knew how it must sound to Clare. It sounded insane to her own ears. How could this be true? Why was the word even coming up in connection with Michael Winters? Half the time she could have sworn she hated the man.

"Oh, honey, no. No, you're not." Clare's words were a flood of denial, and she pulled gently on Jennie's hair, in that listen-to-big-sister way she'd used when they were children. "You've always had a crush on him, honey, that's all. And why not? He's gorgeous to look at—he always has been. And you said yourself he's been putting the rush on you, trying to soften you up that way."

Clare managed a smile, though it was a weak one that didn't quite hide her dismay. "You're not a kid anymore, you know. It's quite normal to work up a full head of steam for a guy like that. But it's not love, honey. Don't forget about Quinn. Or those awful Mitchells."

"I'm not forgetting anything." Jennie felt a wriggle of irritation. Clare had always been able to find the weak point in her little sister's arguments. But she knew it was true— the idea of *loving* Michael when she was willing to suspect him of collusion with the Mitchells was a little crazy.

It went against everything she'd always believed in. Somehow, in her dreams, love was always a blinding flash of certainty. And the man of her dreams was always the paragon of all virtues, worthy in every respect of her adoration.

Now she suddenly saw how utterly childish that had been. Whatever love was, it was much more complicated than that, less like riding off into the cinema sunset, more messy and dark and dangerous. Perhaps, she thought, love meant that, instead of wanting the one you loved to suffer for his sins, you longed to spare him every pain, even the ones he deserved. Maybe it meant you believed that love alone could redeem you, that together you could make a crazy world sane again.

"Maybe this is what love is, Clare," she said impulsively, taking her sister's hand. "Loving in spite of your fears and doubts, in spite of their flaws. Maybe it means that you really *belong* to them somehow, that nothing they do can ever completely turn you against them."

"Or maybe," Clare countered, "it's just that they've got you so hypnotized with their big brown bedroom eyes that you can't see straight." Smiling wryly, she squeezed Jennie's hand, as if to soften the caustic words.

But Jennie, looking into her sister's unhappy blue gaze, had seen the momentary flash of understanding. Clare knew, she suddenly realized. She knew exactly what Jennie was talking about. Clare was caught in the same trap of tormenting ambivalence.

"What about Alex?" Jennie questioned softly. "You still love him no matter what, don't you?"

Clare tried to shake her head, but tears welled up in her beautiful eyes, and somehow the shake turned awkwardly into a nod. And then the both of them were hugging, holding each other tightly, like two drowning people clutching hopelessly in a storm. "Yes, I do," Clare said on a small sob. "God help us both, Jennie. I really do."

FINALLY. Finally she was going home. Michael knew exactly what time it was without even looking at his glowing watch. He'd been checking about every five minutes for approximately a lifetime. It was four-fifteen in the morning. So she hadn't spent the night with Brad McIntosh— not technically—but it was close enough in every way that mattered to Michael.

Over the hours since Brad had led Jennie off the deck, the professor's house had been dark and silent. At first Michael had tortured himself with images of what might be happening behind those walls, but eventually that had become intolerable. So he had turned off his mind, and from that moment on his misery had transformed steadily, dangerously, into a cold block of frozen fury.

Now, as he saw her walking slowly to her car, he powered the Jag's lights with an insolent flick of his wrist. The bright beam caught her in its unblinking trap, and she whipped around, wide-eyed, to face it, frightened hand rising to her throat.

After a moment, she seemed to realize whose car it was. Her hand dropped slowly to her side, and her face hardened. She gave him one long, emotionless stare, during which it was hard to remember that she couldn't see a thing but the glare of his lights, and then she turned away silently. She inserted her key into the door lock, and climbed in, then roared away from the curb with a furious acceleration that nearly stripped her gears.

Spurred on by his anger, he followed without subterfuge, as if his car were chained to hers by the beam of his headlights. But, to his surprise, she didn't go home. She turned toward downtown Houston. She drove fast, too fast, but still he followed. He tailed her aggressively, so close his headlights were like a silver nimbus around her hair. He could even see glimpses of her white, tired face in her rearview mirror.

When she reached the Kearney Building, she parked on the street, and though he was only three paces behind her as she unlocked the front door, she managed to push it shut in his face. He had to use his own key, which Arthur had given him the first night, and by the time he got in she'd already caught an elevator, the double doors shutting in front of her, giving him only a quick glimpse of her set and furious expression.

Flashing his ID to the curious security guard, Michael took the stairs instead, just as glad to have a chance to stretch the kinks out of his cramped legs. He reached the third floor only seconds after the elevator did, in time to see Jennie striding across the dimly lit central work space toward her own office. Silent, blank-faced computers and shrouded typewriters were like gray ghosts all around her, and she moved among them without a sound, hardly seeming to notice them.

The soft thud as she closed her door and the sharp scrape as she twisted the lock reverberated across his already jangled nerves. *No, Jennie,* he thought with grim determination. *It just isn't going to be that easy.*

He had a key, but instead of using it he rapped three times on her office door. Hard. And then three more, even harder. He had raised his hand to knock again when the door suddenly opened a few stingy inches. She stood in the narrow opening, and he could see that her office was still dark behind her.

"Leave me alone, Michael." She looked a little like a ghost herself in the gloom. "I'm just here to do some work. If you want to wait for me, I can't stop you. I haven't even got the energy to try. Just leave me alone."

Her voice had a defeated quality. He could feel her exhaustion and something else, as well, some inner anxiety that revealed itself in a faint tremble behind her words.

"Let me in, Jennie," he said bluntly. He was tired, too, and beyond trying to cushion his words in soft conversational tissue. "We need to talk."

She stared at him, and studying her, he suddenly realized that she was suffering more than mere anxiety. Fear might be a more accurate description, and he felt a moment of shame for the belligerent way he had stalked her here. The skin around her lips and eyes was almost white, like the fragile shell of an egg, but her cheeks looked flushed and feverish. She almost hummed with tension.

"I have work to do." She shifted with a queer, lopsided motion, and looking down, he saw that she had one shoe on and one off. "And there's nothing for us to talk about."

She wouldn't look directly at him. She seemed to be talking to a spot just behind his left ear. He had to suppress the urge to take her face between his hands and move so close she had no choice but to look at him, to acknowledge him, to let him *in,* goddamn it!

Controlling himself required every ounce of discipline he had, but slowly he took the edge of the door in his hand, not really pushing at all, just exerting enough pressure to warn her he could break through whenever he wanted, that she clung to only the illusion of protection. The wood was solid, as expensive as everything else the Kearneys owned, but in his present state it seemed as flimsy as veneer.

"I think there is," he said with quiet warning.

"No." Her eyes glittered with the same fever that sparked fire in her cheeks, and she tightened her hold on the door as if she feared he might try to force his way in. "I'm just too tired tonight, Michael. I'm sorry."

"Damn it, Jennie." His voice was low, but all the frustration of the night was evident in its hoarse intensity. "Talk to me. I'm not going to hurt you."

That got her attention. Her gaze flew to his, and in the single heartbeat of time it took his words to sink in, the blood drained from her face. "All right," she said hollowly, but she didn't back away from the door. "Talk. But make it quick, please. I'm tired."

He believed her—it wasn't just a dodge. She looked tired. Terribly, terribly tired. Her eyes looked bruised, and her shoulders sagged as if she no longer had energy to hold them up.

She looked so fragile. Something burned in his chest, something that felt like pity and threatened his composure. But then he remembered *why* she was so tired, remembered that she'd been in another man's arms all night long, and the burning transmuted into anger.

"You owe me, Jennie." He spoke through gritted teeth. He tightened his fingers over the wood until his knuckles were white. "You know you owe me!"

"Do I?" She raised her brows, his combative tone returning a little of her spirit to her. "For what?"

"For letting you go to Clare."

He could feel his pulse pounding in his fingertips—the door quivered under the intensity of his grip. She looked at it, swallowed hard and then returned her defiant gaze to his. "For *letting* me?"

"That's right," he returned acidly.

He had forgotten how haughty the Kearneys could look when they were angry. Jennie's lids lowered over eyes turned icy, and her brows rose several inches in a delicately disdainful arch. She looked, he realized, a lot like Clare, except that her mouth gave her away. It trembled slightly, though she tried to hide it by tucking one corner in with a vulnerability that Clare had never possessed.

"I don't remember your putting a price on your cooperation," she said, each word quivering with a half-formed frost. "I don't remember agreeing to buy my freedom."

Buy it? He wanted to hit something. He glared at the door, wondering whether pulling it off the hinges would make him feel any better. Damn it, she was deliberately twisting his words.

"I'm not talking about payment, Jennie, and you know it," he said, struggling to stay calm. "I'm talking about trust. I'm talking about gratitude."

The Clare-like sneer vanished, and something more real yet more scathing appeared in its place. An honest anger, a righteous indignation that was typically Jennie had surfaced, and its flame was blistering.

"I refuse to be grateful for the gift of my privacy." Her voice was breaking, and her eyes were glistening with furious tears. "Which you had no right to take away from me in the first place."

"Jennie." He shook his head, his anger backing off a little under the blast of her rage. Where had all this come from? She *had* been grateful, at least at first. She had even seemed to understand, just a little, what a difficult dilemma he found himself in, wanting desperately to please her even though his obligations prohibited it. What had happened to her that could have changed the soft, sequined treasure he had held in his arms into this furious young woman? "Jennie—"

But she wasn't willing to listen. "You think I owe you? Well, all right. I'll pay you with some good advice. Give up. You and my father think Clare is just pulling another dumb stunt, but you're wrong. She ran away from Alex because she's afraid of him. She doesn't trust him, and she's not going back until she finds out what he's really been up to all these years."

He frowned, surprised by her words. All these years? What on earth was Clare imagining? "What do you mean, 'up to'?"

"I thought maybe you already knew," she said, her voice laced with bitterness. "I mean that Alex owes money—a lot of money—to your friends the Mitchells."

That was a sucker punch, and his mind staggered, reeling from the shock. He didn't know exactly what he'd been expecting, but it certainly hadn't been this. He hadn't heard that name in years, but he'd seen their faces in his dreams. The Mitchells. What the hell was Alex doing mixed up with those slimy bastards? Whatever was going on, it was definitely nothing Jennie and Clare should be involved in.

"Listen, Jennie," he said urgently, sliding his fingers down to rest over hers. "If the Mitchells are in this, it could be damned dangerous."

She pulled her arm away, the jerking motion causing the sleeve of her loose cotton dress to slip down over her shoulder. "Well, yes," she said with a grim sarcasm. "That was my point."

"Jennie, if they are in this, you and Clare can't handle it alone. It's crazy to try. You have to get some help."

"We have help." She eyed him coldly, shrugging her shoulder to return her dress to its proper place. "You're not the only private detective in the world, Michael."

"Fine. That's great." He ignored the implicit insult. The thought of Jennie trying to tangle with the likes of the Mitchells made his skin grow cold and clammy. "But let me help, too."

"You?" She laughed, a brittle sound. "You're on the other side, remember? You're already signed up to help my father track Clare down and bring her back." She narrowed her eyes. "And besides, I don't trust you, either."

It wasn't as if he hadn't known that. He'd known it for six years. But somehow, tonight, after everything else that had happened, it was, finally, just too much.

His control slipped like a wild horse darting free of a bit. With a curse, he shoved the door open with his shoulder and, reaching in, grabbed her by both arms.

"Why, damn it?" He was so angry and so incredibly hurt that he could hardly speak coherently. *"Why?"*

Staring at him numbly, she didn't answer, and somehow her silence enraged him more. "Why?" He wanted to shake her. "I'm sick to death of your veiled insults, Jennie. Just come out with it. Why do you hate me so much? What the hell do you think I'm guilty of?"

"Guilty of?" She looked confused. "Oh, I don't know. I guess I just wonder...." Her voice was strange, the stilted monotone completely unlike her usual melodic pitch, and she seemed oblivious to his angry hands on her already bruised arms. "I guess I wonder where you got the money to start your detective agency. Clare tells me you're a very big deal up there in Seattle. She doesn't think all that elegance could possibly have come from Quinn's insurance money."

"Get to the point." He almost choked on the words. What the hell did Clare know about it?

"Okay. I guess the point is—how much money do *you* owe the Mitchell family?"

Something red burst in front of his eyes, and his head began to swim with a painful, swirling fury. Owe the— His fingers tightened until he could feel her slender bones beneath her flesh. What kind of stinking garbage had Clare been filling Jennie's mind with?

"None," he managed to say, though his brain felt like it was on fire, and his teeth were clenched so tightly his jaw ached. "What kind of a damn fool question is that? Owe those sleazy crooks? Not one red cent."

Her expression didn't change. It was still equal measures fear, misery and a faraway numbness, as if his denial had bounced off her closed mind unheeded.

"And why is that?" She sounded like someone in a trance, and he wondered wildly if he should slap her, to try to bring her out of it before she could say something unforgivable. "Could it be because *they* owed you? Owed you for doing them a great big favor?"

"Are you crazy, Jennie? Has Clare been making you absolutely crazy? What has she been telling you? Why are you listening to her? What favor could I possibly do those men?"

For answer, Jennie just shook her head, over and over, as though it weren't fully under her control. It was a mute, anguished denial, as if her thoughts were just too horrible to accept. Two tears slipped out of her unseeing eyes, dislodged by the motion, and fell in silver trails down her cheeks.

And then he knew. God help him, he knew what she was thinking. *Don't say it, Jennie,* a desperate voice cried inside his throbbing head. *Don't say it.*

But she did. With a voice drowning in tears, she said the words she must have been thinking for six years.

"You could have agreed to make sure my brother was alone at the warehouse that night. Alone, so that there would be only one witness." A sob broke loose from deep in her throat, the sound of a million silver tears waiting to be shed. "Only one witness to kill."

CHAPTER TEN

As HER WORDS ECHOED in the empty air, Michael dropped her arms as if his hands had suddenly gone too numb to grip. He backed away, the anger dying out of his eyes abruptly, and stared at her through the murky light with a stunned expression, as if she had turned into a stranger.

Ironically, her emotions seemed at that instant to burst into a new, intense life, and she was overcome with horror at what she'd said. Both hands flew to her burning cheeks, and she choked out a small, dismayed groan.

Good God, what had she been thinking, to let such an accusation cross her lips? She had never intended to confront him with her suspicions, knowing it would be worse than pointless. If the suspicions were true, naturally he would never, ever admit it. And if they were not true...

If they were not true, then what she had said was unforgivable. It had sounded so plausible when she and Clare had discussed it. Every detail had seemed so suspicious—Michael's fortuitous absence on the night of Quinn's death, his silence about what had happened that night, his sudden departure from Texas and inexplicable rise to wealth after the robbery, and finally his willingness to help her father find Clare. The three young men had once been the closest of friends. If Alex was still having shady dealings with the Mitchells, then why not Michael, too?

But like a subtle color that seems to change from green to blue and back again, everything looked different when she was with Michael. Here, in the power of his presence, she could see that Clare's "evidence" was nothing but fears and prejudices stacked on top of each other, creating a fearsome shadow she and Clare had run from, mistaking the shadow for the monster, the suspicion for proof.

And what about the evidence of her senses? When she was with Michael, her dominant sensation was always desire, and the only fear she felt was the fear that she would fall completely under his spell.

Take tonight. Her nerves on edge after being with Clare, Jennie had not wanted to return to the ranch, where she and Michael would be alone on the second floor, locked in a vulnerable intimacy. Beyond the house, acre after deserted acre stretched out, and her ill father and his timid nurse offered no protection. So instead she had fled to the Kearney Building, where, thanks to her father's security phobia, watchmen guarded every floor, ready to spring to her defense if she pushed one small button.

Yet now that she was here, alone in her dark office with Michael, Jennie realized that, though she was still afraid, she was not afraid of *him*. Somehow that one fact seemed more significant than any "logical" deduction Clare could ever make.

But what now? While she stood there, muddled, searching for something to say that would undo the damage, he'd left her. He stood across the room, looking down onto the bleak street below. A lone street lamp cast confusing stripes through the open mini blinds, rendering his expression unreadable.

"My father died when I was six," he said suddenly, the sound of his voice slicing through the thick silence that had accumulated in the gloom. "My mother was a mess after that. She lived with one man after another—half a dozen of them at least, before I finally left when I was sixteen."

Jennie frowned, surprised both by the information and by his sudden launch into a personal history. What did this have to do with Quinn? Was he going to explain why the Mitchell money had been such a temptation? Was he finally, after all these years, going to break his silence?

"Some of the boyfriends were worse than others. The best I could hope for was to be ignored. When I was little, I used to practice being invisible, not moving a muscle for hours, and barely breathing at all, so that they wouldn't notice me when they came in drunk or stoned or—" Michael's hand twitched, as if to brush away the memory "—or whatever."

He might have been talking to himself. He still stared down at the empty street, his back to Jennie. And his tone was musing, contemplative rather than defensive, as if he was merely trying to sort things out in his mind.

"I didn't dare make any mistakes. A C in math could leave me black and blue. A chore left undone could knock out my front teeth. My diligence impressed the hell out of my teachers, so when I left home it was easy to find a job. Two jobs, in fact, so I could pay the rent while I finished high school. Then I joined the Army."

The Army. Jennie remembered how achingly handsome Michael had been in his uniform. His tall, muscular darkness had been the perfect foil to Quinn's lithe golden grace, and together they had taken every woman's breath away.

She swallowed a sharp lump that blocked her throat, but she didn't say a word, knowing that the slightest sound could interrupt his semiconscious flow of memories. And she wanted to hear everything, every word he was willing to tell her. She had never known, had never really cared, where Michael came from. It hadn't seemed important to her at the time, though now she saw how wrong she had been, how completely his past had defined him.

He was quiet for a long, maddening moment, but she bit back the impulse to prompt him. He would get to the point of this in his own time, in his own way.

"I met Quinn in the Army. I could tell right away that he didn't belong there. I even guessed that he was just there to spite his father. Rich kids like to do that, don't they?" Jennie thought she saw a smile twist one corner of his mouth, but it might have been a trick of the shifting light.

"Quinn was always in trouble, always pulling some stunt that would land him, and sometimes the rest of us, in hot water. But he was so damned charming that nobody really minded." Michael shook his head, as if helpless to explain Quinn. "Everybody loved him."

He took a deep breath and ran a finger along the blinds, which gave off a restless metallic rattle. "I'm not really sure why we became such good friends. Attraction of opposites, I guess. He was amused by my ability to stay out of trouble... and I—" he drew another long breath, as if his lungs were running through oxygen too fast "—I hadn't ever met anyone so audacious. He made life seem like such an exciting game. I'd never had much fun before, not that kind. I think I went a little crazy."

Jennie took a couple of steps closer to him but, encased in his memories, Michael didn't seem to notice.

"And then he invited me to go home with him for Christmas. He knew I didn't have anywhere else to go. If I'd gone to my mother's house, I might have killed the guy who was living with her. I owed him. He was a really sick guy, and I—" He broke off. "Anyway, then I met your family. Arthur welcomed me like a son, Clare was just as exciting as Quinn, and you—"

Jennie held her breath. Michael turned his head slightly, looking at her, one side of his face in complete shadow. "You thought I was wonderful. You were just a kid, really, and you probably would have worshipped any older guy who came into your world, but I loved it. It was like a drug, all that adoration, and pretty soon I was addicted."

She opened her mouth to say something, to say how she, too, had grown addicted to the sight of him, to his dark, rugged earthiness, so exotic in her overcivilized world, to his aura of invincible strength, both of will and of body. But to her disappointment he turned his head away.

"Unfortunately I was addicted to other things, too," he said bitterly. "To Quinn's carefree approach to life. To staying up late playing cards and flirting with every woman in sight. To sleeping late and drinking too much and playing hooky from my responsibilities. Quinn made it seem so easy to get away with all that, and I was so hungry for fun that I followed him blindly down the old yellow brick road."

Jennie, who was listening intently to every nuance of Michael's voice, heard the sharpening of self-loathing with a sense of surprise. Did Michael really believe he had been so wicked? She remembered him as frequently providing the voice of sanity, managing somehow to keep Quinn from carrying out several of his more harebrained ideas.

Suddenly, like an alarm, the intercom buzzed loudly. Jennie's heart lurched at the unexpected sound, and then she recognized it. The security guard. Inwardly she cursed the man's terrible timing. Now that they'd been interrupted, would Michael ever finish his story?

She hurried to the desk and pressed the button. "Yes?"

An odd, electronic voice rose over the static. "Everything all right, Miss Kearney?"

"Fine, George." She forced herself to be polite. "Thanks. I'll be working for a while. No need to check in."

With a quick motion she flipped the intercom's switch to off. Then she went to the office door and, without a word of explanation, locked it. Michael watched her silently.

Turning away from the door, she met his gaze with as much equilibrium as she could find. At least now he'd know she trusted him.

But it didn't seem to make him any happier. In fact, suddenly he seemed less like a man in a trance, more like a man in a cage—nervous, edgy and restless. He moved away from the window, prowling through the room as he spoke, touching chair backs and lampshades, shifting magazines and pencils. Jennie stood still, following his restive progress with her gaze.

He stopped in front of a picture of Quinn that sat on her bookcase. "I've known since I was six that people don't ever really get away with anything. I should have seen that the yellow brick road didn't lead to Oz—it was just another dead-end street."

He scowled at her brother's ever-smiling face. "Damn it, I should have known the Mitchells were paying too much for that warehouse security job. And why did they want a trio of inexperienced bozos like us to play night watchmen, anyway? But it was so tempting to shut off that annoying voice in my head. It was easy money. Besides, I had other things on my mind."

He tore his gaze away from the picture. "Alex already had his eye on Clare, but Quinn and I had just met Brooke and her roommate." He shook his head. "God, we really thought we'd been given the key to the fun house. They were so experienced, so sophisticated, so full of life, and they thought private detectives were glamorous."

Prowling again, he picked up a magazine, and without looking at it tossed it onto the coffee table so hard it skidded onto the floor. His voice toughened. "I was twenty-three, but suddenly I had the self-control of a sixteen-year-old. Brooke and her friend lived in a third-floor walk-up just a few blocks from the warehouse. Stairway to heaven, we called it. We thought that was very funny."

A small hurt sound brushed past Jennie's lips, but if Michael heard it he ignored it, bent on finishing the ugly story. Her hands behind her back, Jennie grabbed the edge of the desk, tightening her shoulders and squaring her feet as if bracing herself for a high wind. She would listen to all of it. All of it. No matter how much it hurt.

"Alex watched during the day, and Quinn and I alternated nights—he'd go there Monday while I watched the warehouse, then Tuesday would be my turn. It went on like that for about a week. And then one night, probably at the very moment when I was in bed with Brooke, someone broke into the warehouse." He picked up a glass paperweight, and both hands closed around it as his voice thickened. "They broke in, and they found Quinn there. Alone. And they killed him."

"Michael," she said, finally finding her voice under a suffocating layer of tears. It didn't sound like her voice at all, but it would have to do. "Michael, it could just as easily have been you." She hadn't ever heard that Quinn had left the warehouse, too. Michael must never have told anyone, not even the police, or it would have come out during the inquest. His silence had been absolute, and it had allowed the Kearney family to maintain the fiction of Quinn's martyrdom.

"It could have happened on a night when he was gone, instead. And then it would have been you—" Her voice broke, and she shuddered convulsively, imagining his blood pouring out, imagining Quinn covered with Michael's blood.

"But it *wasn't!*" Michael crossed the room in three violent strides, until he was right in front of her, his hands clenched at his side. "Don't you think I've wished a thousand times that it had been? Don't you think I've replayed it all in my head till I go mad, trying to get back to that night so that I could tell Brooke no? Or so that I could decide to leave Brooke's apartment sooner? To get back to the warehouse in time?''

His voice was rough with emotion. ''I don't know exactly what happened that night, Jennie. I don't know if it was the Mitchell brothers or just some thugs off the street. But I know I could have helped Quinn if I'd been there to back him up. If only I hadn't been so hell-bent on my own pleasure, on indulging my selfish needs one more time—''

''Stop, Michael, please! I don't want to hear about that.'' She put the palm of her hand across his lips. The mental pictures were already too vivid, and she felt lacerated with pain at the thought of Michael loving another woman. One more time... Something tore at her insides, and the pain was unendurable.

''Well, it's true,'' he said, moving her hand roughly aside. ''I was a bastard, Jennie, and Quinn was punished for it.'' He didn't relinquish her hand. He kept it prisoner in an iron-cold grip at his side. ''But I was punished for it, too. I got Brooke pregnant that night. I didn't love her, I never loved her, but I got her pregnant. So I married her, and I tried to learn to love her, and I waited for the baby that would give me a reason to go on with the farce my life had become.''

He squeezed her hand so hard she felt the bones press together, but she didn't flinch. She didn't pull away. It was a desperate clutch of intolerable pain, and she was glad to be the one who received his suffering. She was sure there was no child, and she wondered whether Brooke the Beautiful Bimbo, living up to her nickname, had deliberately lied to him.

''And then, when Brooke was six months pregnant, a truck smashed into her car. Everyone was killed. The truck driver, Brooke—" he groaned and tilted his head back, the moonlight glimmering off the hint of wetness on his dark, long lashes "—and my son."

Jennie choked on the breath she tried to take, inhaling helpless tears along with air. She prayed a wordless apology to Brooke for misjudging her, and then the prayer turned into an entreaty that the agony she glimpsed would somehow be eased.

"Oh, God," she whispered, putting her other hand to his cheek, tracing the path taken by one scalding tear. "Oh, Michael."

"So you see I have paid, Jennie." He opened his eyes and stared into hers with a lost and hazed expression. "I know it's no more than I deserve, but I wanted you to know that I've paid, too. And I go on paying, just as you and your father and Clare do. I know it's not enough...."

"Hush," she pleaded, stroking his damp hair from his burning forehead. "It *is* enough. It's too much."

"No—" he began, but she silenced him with a kiss.

It was not meant to be a sexual connection. It was meant to be soothing, a blessing and a forgiveness. But when her lips touched his, something else was there, too, something inescapably sensual, a whisper that said souls could sometimes find one another through the body, that physical loving could be a benediction, too.

She drank in the sensation for a long moment, and then drew back slowly. "It's over, Michael," she said solemnly. "All the pain is over now."

He shook his head mutely, his eyes dry and disbelieving but searching her face, as if he was looking for something that could change his mind.

"Yes," she said. "Now it's time for us to heal each other."

His mouth twisted. "I don't think that's possible."

"Yes, it is." She opened her eyes wider, hoping he could see into her heart. "Make love to me."

A ripple of tension sped through his body, from his cheek where her hand rested to his legs that were so close to hers she could feel the heat of them through her skirt.

"Jennie—"

"Please," she said. "I've wanted you for so long." She tunneled her fingers into his hair. "Oh, Michael, you could have had me back then, you know. You didn't have to go to Brooke."

"I know," he said harshly, moving closer with a low groan, close enough that their bodies lightly touched. "But you were seventeen, Jennie. And so innocent." He touched her chin. "There were some sins even I wasn't devil enough to commit."

"Then take me now," she whispered. "I'm not a child anymore."

He almost smiled, his fingers trailing from her chin to her throat, where he found and touched the pulse that beat wildly. "Yes, I know," he murmured. His hand drifted farther down, and a shiver of anticipation prickled across her skin.

Touch me. Something that wasn't quite words spoke in her head, and hearing the thrill, she closed her eyes, tilting her head back in waiting acquiescence. *Touch me.*

But he didn't. He flattened his hand across her collarbone, just above her breast, as if to feel the throbbing of her heart, as though he sought some kind of answer from the heavy drumbeat there.

"I don't know— I don't know if I can be what you want me to be, Jennie," he said in a rough undertone, as if the words were hard to force free. "It's been—difficult. Since Brooke... Since Quinn."

What was he trying to tell her? Surely he wasn't trying to deny the physical potency of his body. It was too late to suggest such a thing. His body was close enough to hers that she knew he wanted her, and the pure masculine force of that desire made her dizzy, eager for the completion it promised.

Something else, then. But what? She lowered her head and opened her eyes, knowing that all the sweet urgency she felt was shining in them. She heard him, but the words seemed so unimportant. Whatever had happened before was going to be meaningless in this new and wonderful world they were about to discover. If only she could make him see that.

"I might disappoint you," he said slowly. "I'm not able to—quite abandon myself. Do you understand? I just don't feel pleasure, not anymore." He looked at his hand, as if it belonged to someone else. "Guilt is a strange thing, Jennie. It gets in the way."

"Not tonight," she said softly, and taking his hand in hers, she guided it slowly to her breast. She pressed his palm against the puckered tip, sighing as his warmth flooded into her. "Tonight nothing can come between us."

He wanted to believe her. But even as he touched the rounded curve of her breast, he felt himself closing up. Like a man who has wanted and been denied for so long he had finally taught himself not to want at all, his brain rejected the sensations his nerves were sending him.

His hand hurt, as if an electrical current had short-circuited in his palm. He put his other hand on her desperately, trying to force himself to feel. This, this *deadness* was how, as a child, he had coped with cruelty, turning his emotions off like a tap. This was how he had endured physical pain, by making his unhappy body belong to someone else. But, until the night Quinn died while Michael made love to Brooke, the deadness had never affected his love-making.

Once he'd known how to make love, how to feel love. He had to find a way back to that. He couldn't be dead tonight. Not tonight. Not with Jennie.

With awkward fingers he pulled free a dozen tiny pearl buttons and found her naked skin, ivory in the moonlight, rising and falling with her shallow breaths.

He slid his fingers inside the lace of her bra and, cupping his hands around her, groaned helplessly. He knew the sensitive peaks were tightening beneath his fingers, knew that she was shivering under his touch, but he didn't really feel it. He knew hot waves were breaking over her, and he, too, should have been caught up in that tide. Instead he stood, like the watcher on the shore, alone and aching and full of a dry, hopeless pain.

Desperate tension coiled his muscles, and paradoxically, he couldn't have been physically any readier. He knew from wretched experience that he could take her now, could drive into her with a force and a power that would make her cry out with pleasure. He could make it last forever, if she wanted, could service her like a machine until she was weeping in his arms.

And then, when he sensed she was tired, he could take his own release with a steely indifference that was chilling to his soul. And, unless she was extremely observant, she wouldn't notice anything amiss. He would make the appropriate moves, but his climax would be an emotionless reaction, like a reflex. Not even one single stray goose bump would rise on his skin. He would feel nothing. Nothing but a supreme emptiness and a savage despair.

But, though her small, whimpering noises were asking him to do just that, he wasn't sure he could. Not with Jennie. *Please,* he begged his tense, dead hands. *Not like this with Jennie.*

His hands would not comply. And he knew he couldn't leave her unsatisfied, on fire with a wanting he remembered well even if he could no longer feel its flame. He would help her find the pleasure she deserved, and he would try to find his own happiness in hers.

Still, it was with a bitter sense of failure that he moved his hands lower, to where her hips were shifting against his in a semiconscious urging. The rest of the buttons fell away under his touch, and then he lifted her up onto the edge of the desk. She buried her face in his shoulder, making low, frantic sounds as he feathered his fingers slowly up the inner edge of her thighs, until they reached the center of her.

She gasped into his shoulder, kneading his arms with the untutored rhythm her body instinctively understood. Slipping past the meager barrier of her lacy panties, he found his way easily inside her, guided by the warm throbbing of her desire, and in only seconds he could feel the first tiny tremors close around his fingers.

He slowed down, knowing he had to be careful. She was poised for the fall, like a tightrope walker on a shifting, swaying rope, holding on to her balance with sheer will. His fingers, so experienced in this giving of pleasure, could, with one nudge of carefully placed pressure, topple her. But he wanted to wait. He wanted to take her higher first. He wanted to take her as high as she could go, and then, only then, he would send her spiraling through the empty air, crying and falling and spinning with a fearful delight.

She murmured fretfully as he took his hand away, but with soothing noises he calmed her, stroking her hair and her back until he felt the tension recede just enough. Then, scooping her into his arms, he carried her to the sofa and laid her there.

He sat beside her, letting her legs drape across his lap while he slid her shoes off, his hands stroking the high, sensitive arch of each foot as he did so. Pulling her to a half-sitting position, he slowly eased free her dress and bra. Then he gently pressed against her shoulders, and she lay back again. She didn't protest, but, crossing both hands over her naked breasts, she began to tremble as he trailed his fingers down the plane of her stomach.

Her eyes were deep pools of navy blue, bigger and more luminous than any eyes he had ever seen. She kept them fixed on his face, as if he was the stable center of a frightening universe, while he slowly slipped the last lacy scrap of clothing down her legs.

She was so beautiful, her skin glowing in the moonlight with the iridescent sheen of pearls. But before he allowed himself to touch her, he took off his clothes quickly and sorted through the discarded items. He hated, somehow, for her to see the small foil packet, hated for her to think he had brought it along expecting her easy surrender. The truth was he had never, not for one minute of the past six years, been without a contraceptive, however unlikely its use had seemed. That was one lesson he didn't need to learn twice.

Without speaking, she watched him put it on, her breath coming ever faster. Then, when the rapid, shallow sounds told him she wasn't going to be able to wait much longer, he knelt between her legs. Though designed on soft, generous lines, the sofa had not been built for lovemaking, and there was just enough space for him to place his hands on either side of her. To help make room, she wrapped her legs around his back, and as their positions settled into a perfect fit, she gasped slightly. He knew she could feel the ready promise of his body against hers.

"Michael...." A soft blush rose in her cheeks. Through it all, her eyes had never left his, and their blue depths were suddenly brimming with tears. "Michael, I do love you so much."

Her voice trembled with undisguised vulnerability, and the sound reached deep inside him, unbalancing him. He stared at her for a long moment and then, with suddenly shaking fingers, he touched her cheek.

"Oh, God, Jennie." What could he say to such an unguarded declaration? What answer could guilt have for such innocence? But it must have been enough, because, shutting her eyes as if in immense relief, she smiled.

Such a simple thing, a smile... And yet that tremulous expression of pure faith set off a reaction in him that was amazingly intense, like an inner earthquake. Everything shifted. And then something hard and heavy inside him was shoved aside, something that had been blocking the once-bubbling spring of his emotions, a spring that had frozen from disuse.

He caught his breath, unable to believe. The sensation trickled slowly at first, just a tiny, shivering ripple, as if, still sluggish and half-thawed, it couldn't believe it really was free to flow.

But even that small rivulet of feeling was a miracle to him. And he knew that Jennie, his beautiful Jennie, was the miracle. She trusted him—trusted him to take her with tenderness and to protect the love she offered him so freely. It was perhaps the absolution he had given up hoping for.

His eyes were hot and stinging as he slowly lowered his mouth to her shoulder. He was almost afraid to touch her, afraid that somehow her soft forgiveness was just a dream, that she would instead have the hard, cool, unyielding quality of the pearls he had moments ago likened her to.

But she was warm. She was Jennie. He groaned his relief, his gratitude, into her neck, burying his face in her hair and kissing the sunshine of her skin, where a hot pulse beat madly under his lips. She was as warm and liquid as a summer ocean, and suddenly he was aching all over, wanting with a blind urgency to dive into her, to immerse his frozen soul in the sweet heat.

"I love you," she said again, this time with a frantic breathlessness, lifting her body up to his. He could no longer stop himself. With his mouth, with his hands, he touched her everywhere, absorbing her warmth through every nerve ending, glorying in the melting swell that coursed through his veins, washing past his defenses like a river overflowing its banks.

"Oh, Jennie, yes," he cried, drowning. "Love me."

She obeyed instantly, running her hands down the length of his back, from shoulders to hips. And then, with fingers that seemed to tremble with wonder and need, she traced the tightly muscled hollows of his buttocks. He arced painfully, bending his head to her breast, and, moaning, she squeezed him closer, pressing her legs against him hungrily.

He was lost, swept into the current. Whispering her name, he closed his eyes and focused on the awesome pain of being consumed by passion. Of being alive. Of being in love.

When she brought her trembling fingers around and guided him into her, he didn't resist. He tried to remember his part, tried to find the competent rhythm he had once controlled with ease. But his body was no longer his own.

If his movements were made awkward by his primal desperation, hers were more graceful. Her legs anchored him, and with her hands on his thighs she brought him home, again and again, until wild, hot currents of pure, screaming pleasure swept through him.

"Jennie!" Even when he called out hoarsely, she didn't stop. He heard her agonized moan, felt her fingers tighten convulsively, and the currents began to double in on themselves, crashing silently over him, buffeting his body, until a profound surge roiled through him.

"Jennie, please!" But she wouldn't let him escape, and with one last, disbelieving cry, his soul finally shot free of the riptide and exploded in a blessed, incandescent geyser of molten joy.

CHAPTER ELEVEN

AT FIRST, half awake and fuzzy-minded, Jennie was confused—confused by the strange stripe of light that lay on the floor, by the rough fabric under her cheek where her satin pillowcase should have been, but most of all by the combination of bruised exhaustion and sensual languor that dominated her body.

Stretching thoughtlessly, she encountered something with her feet, and she lifted up on one elbow, squinting into the half-light. The arm of a sofa. Her office sofa...

And then, lying back with a long, low sigh of pure happiness, she was confused no longer. Last night, in this office, on this sofa, she and Michael had made love. She brought her knees up to her chest, as if to hug the memory closer. Made love. In a way, the words were too small, too ordinary, to encompass what had happened here last night.

Like a camera gradually focusing, her thoughts began to clear. What time was it? She snuggled under her cotton covering, then, looking down at the blue sprigs of flowers, realized what it was. Her dress. Michael must have draped it over her at some point—though she was still naked under it, a fact she found both disconcerting and strangely erotic.

She turned her gaze quickly to the large windows that looked out onto the central office. The blinds were closed tightly, she saw with relief, but she could hear the mild hum of voices that said the office outside was definitely awake. Thank goodness she had locked the door last night.

But where was Michael? She sat up, somehow getting her arms into the sleeves of the dress without ever quite baring herself. She began closing the long row of buttons as she stood and looked around the empty room. His clothes were gone—there was, oddly, no sign that he'd ever been there at all. She stifled a prickle of anxiety. Probably he'd awakened first and headed for the executive lounge to pull himself together.

The hands of her wall clock said eight o'clock. Shocked that she could have fallen into such a deep sleep that she was oblivious to the arrival of the staff, she straightened her dress, hoping it wasn't apparent that she wore no underclothes.

She slipped her feet into the shoes that sat side by side near the sofa, and combing her fingers through her tousled hair, she went to the office window. Lifting one slat, she peeked through the blinds.

Only four or five early birds milled about, mostly perched against the edges of desks, drinking coffee and chatting. One of the programmers was trying to fly paper airplanes into his wastebasket. Obviously they didn't suspect that the boss was in her office. Jennie smiled, feeling pleasantly risqué. They certainly would never have guessed that the boss had been making love on the office sofa.

A movement from the art department at the back of the room caught her eye, and she peered, trying to make out details. No one should be in there yet, but a man who stood with his back to her was unfolding a large map on a drawing board.

Her first instinct was the agreeable assumption that it must be Michael—no one on her staff, artist or otherwise, was that tall and trim and muscular—but then she frowned, noticing that the man had on a green sportshirt and faded jeans. That wasn't what Michael had been wearing last night.

And why would Michael be over there anyway, in a separate office, looking at a map? Her mind, shying away from the most obvious answer, tossed alternatives at her wildly. The man must be someone else. From another department. A client. A friend of an employee, a brother, a husband...

She widened the gap in the blinds and willed the man to turn around.

He didn't. Instead he smoothed the map on the table and bent over to study it.

Jennie's eyes widened, and her hands balled into fists. She knew that back, those wide shoulders that spread even wider as the man leaned on the heels of his hands. Last night her hands had memorized every corded muscle in that back, had absorbed through her fingertips a permanent imprint of the shape and texture of him.

It was Michael. Up early, freshly dressed, eager to go to work. Her mouth suddenly tasted of ashes. Oh, how practical he was. He thought of everything, didn't he? A change of clothes, a condom... She felt an absurd urge to laugh, or perhaps to cry, thinking how confident he must have been when he came here last night. And now that he had gotten what he wanted he was back to business. He'd even brought along his own map.

Just then Stephanie, her secretary, rapped on the window to the art office, and Michael turned, a questioning smile on his face. Jennie's heart dove into the pit of her stomach. Even now, even across the yards of office that separated them, that smile had the power to melt the very core of her.

Stephanie looked fairly affected, too. Smoothing her hair self-consciously, she chattered something Jennie couldn't hear and she handed Michael a small batch of papers. He gave Stephanie another smile, as if pleased with the delivery, and Stephanie responded with a laugh loud enough to just penetrate Jennie's office.

Jennie let the blinds fall into place, her head aching as she tried to sort out what she had seen. But she couldn't think logically. Every time she'd start to lay the facts out in a neat row, some new emotion would sweep through like an unruly wind and scatter them. Love disrupted anger, shame displaced trust, fear overturned hope. With a frustrated groan she plopped onto the sofa, her fingers pressed against her pounding temples, and wished she could just run away from the whole bewildering mess. Maybe Clare had had the right idea.

Jennie's office adjoined her secretary's, and after a couple of minutes Jennie heard Stephanie pattering on the computer keyboard. Jennie stood up with sudden decision, went to the window to peek one more time at Michael, who thankfully was still bent over his map, and then tiptoed to Stephanie's door. It, too, was locked—obviously Michael's doing. He was very thorough, wasn't he? Jennie wondered bitterly how much experience he'd had with office interludes.

Stephanie looked up with an astonished expression.

"Miss Kearney! Where did you come from? I didn't know you were in yet."

Jennie made no effort to explain what was, essentially, inexplicable. She merely motioned Stephanie closer and spoke in a voice so low it was almost a whisper.

"What is Michael Winters doing in the art department?" she asked, careful not to sound accusatory. Stephanie had a tendency to ramble with defensive fervor whenever she detected a hint of reproach in her boss's voice.

But this time Stephanie was clearly too curious to worry about possible criticism. She frowned quizzically and lowered her voice to a whisper, too.

"I don't really know," she said. "Mr. Kearney told us that Mr. Winters was to have the run of the office, so I didn't think it was my place to ask." She looked over her shoulder, obviously enjoying the little intrigue. "Why? Do you think he's doing something he shouldn't?"

Jennie shrugged, again unwilling to explain. "You delivered some papers to him a minute ago," she said. "Do you know what they were?"

Stephanie shook her head ruefully, as if disappointed that she hadn't been a better spy. "Something from his office in Seattle, that's all I know. Looked like a list of addresses. It was faxed, so it must have been important." Her eyes lit up behind her glasses. "I know! He's got it spread out all over the drawing board, along with a bunch of Houston-area street maps. Want me to go out there and try to get a look at it?"

"No." Addresses. Street maps. Jennie's last hopes slipped and fell with a crash. "No, it doesn't really matter."

Shutting her eyes, she rested her head against the door jamb. She didn't need the details. Even an emotion-wrecked mind could slip these facts into the appropriate slots. He was still hunting for Clare. Nothing that had happened last night had altered his determination to see this job through.

Jennie played back the entire night in her head, in a jumpy fast-forward that skipped over the more disturbing physical memories. He hadn't ever promised her, even by implication, that he'd abandon the search. They hadn't talked about Clare at all.

So she had only herself to blame. Wasn't this what he had warned her about? That, if they made love before they talked things through, the morning after would be full of ugly recriminations? Wasn't that really as good as saying she shouldn't expect too much from a purely sexual encounter?

And—worst of all—when she reconstructed everything with hindsight's cruel clarity, she saw that there was one glaring blank spot in the dialogue. She might have been too swept away by passion to notice it then, but this morning it was as conspicuous as if a spotlight was trained on it.

He had never said he loved her. Not once. Not even to help her dress slide more easily from her shoulders, as certain kinds of men were infamous for doing. And not even when she had, completely unbidden, spilled the secrets of her heart, like a child dropping her worthless treasures at his feet.

"I love you," she had told him. And he had said nothing.

"Stephanie, I've got to get out of here without Michael knowing it," Jennie said, opening her eyes. Even today's disillusionment was easier to face than last night's folly.

Stephanie was staring at her, a worried frown creasing her forehead. "Are you okay?" she asked doubtfully.

Jennie nodded, trying to pull herself together. "I'm fine, but I do need a favor. Do you think you could keep him occupied long enough to let me get away safely?"

The frown smoothed itself out as Stephanie grinned. "It would be my pleasure."

Winking slyly, she grabbed one of the empty coffee cups she kept in the supply cupboard and hurried into the main office. Jennie, watching from her office window, had to smile at the sight of Stephanie's plump figure bearing down on the art department with the unswervable determination of a small tornado.

Her smile faded quickly, though, as, casting a glance around the room to check for telltale signs of last night's insanity, she noticed that her underclothes had been neatly folded on the table next to the sofa. At the sight, heat flooded through her body as she felt again the drag of lace over her thighs. Oh, Michael . . .

Impulsively she grabbed a sheet of notepaper. *Had to see Clare,* she scribbled. *Maybe we can talk later.* Then she snatched up her underclothes, stuffed them in her purse— she'd dress at Clare's—and left the note in their place.

A sarcastic inner voice mocked the idiotically hopeful tone of the note. Talk? Talk about what? When he realized that she'd sneaked out, he'd be furious, just as she'd been furious to see him studying a map. They were back to the beginning, it seemed, in this chess game she'd hoped might become a relationship. *Fool,* the voice scoffed. *Won't you ever learn?*

Scooping up her purse, she hurried through Stephanie's office to the supply room, from there to the service stair-well, and, looking over her shoulder the whole time, from there to her car. She forced the berating inner voice to be quiet. All the self-loathing and misery could—and un-doubtedly would—come later. Right now she was already an hour late, and she didn't have time for a broken heart.

MICHAEL TOOK a sip of the coffee Stephanie had brought him and, flicking another look toward Jennie's shuttered office, forced his attention back to the maps. He told him-self he was glad Jennie was getting some sleep, but his body was saying something else. He was restless, tense with the bone-deep desire to go in there, to wake her up with a long, slow kiss, to toss aside the soft cotton dress he'd covered her with, to make love to her with all the concentration and self-control he'd been unable to find last night.

A ripple of heat shivered through him, all the way down to his toes, and the lines on the map suddenly swam before his eyes. He blinked hard and forced himself to focus. Let her sleep. He had locked both entrances, and he'd left his copy of the key on her desk, a gesture of faith that he hoped she'd understand. She could get out whenever she wanted, but he couldn't get in until she invited him.

He smiled stupidly at the map of coastal islands, seeing Jennie's face where the lines and letters were supposed to be. She would let him in—he didn't doubt it for a minute. There was no arrogance in his certainty. He knew he didn't deserve her. But he also knew that she was his.

Again that thrill stirred within him, as if, now that his senses were awakened, he existed in a constant state of awareness. He wondered if she even suspected the miracle she'd worked last night when she had said she loved him. He closed his eyes, hearing the soft words. It was as if he had been falling for years, falling into some hopeless, bottomless pit of despair. And then she had handed him wings.

He knotted his hand in his hair, trying to drag himself back to reality. It sounded quite noble to talk about gratitude, but frankly, if he didn't get hold of all this rampaging gratitude, he was going to have to go over and break her damn door down.

He sneaked another look at his watch. Only eight. He'd promised himself he'd let her sleep until ten, which still would give her only about four hours of rest. The dawn had already begun to stain the room a pinkish gold when Jennie had spooned her warm body against his and, using his arm for a pillow, fallen asleep in his embrace.

A slow burn rose from deep in the muscles of his legs as he remembered how small the sofa had been, how tightly she had tucked herself up against him, the subtle curves of her bottom fitting perfectly into him, so perfectly that, though he was only semiconscious and unimaginably spent, a quiver of desire had coursed through his exhausted body.

He shifted, dragging in a steadying breath. Ten o'clock was still two hours away. Maybe, he decided with shameless selfishness, nine would be late enough.

But even one hour seemed like forever. He had to stop this, had to wrench his mind away from thoughts of how she felt, how she smelled, how she tasted...

Well, that's what the maps were for. He stared glumly at the list of recent rentals Lisa had faxed him, wishing, as he had been wishing for an hour now, that he could get lucky and stumble onto some clue. How he would love to spare Jennie the misery of having to decide between him and Clare! He knew in his heart that, after last night, Jennie would tell him whatever he wanted to know. They were way past the cat-and-mouse phase. They were lovers. Still, he knew Jennie. She'd never forgive herself if she betrayed her sister's trust. And he knew Clare, too, he thought with a grimace. She'd never let Jennie forget it, either.

But, if he could discover the address on his own, it could solve everything. If he already knew where Clare was, Jennie wouldn't have to tell him.

But he was halfway through the five-page list, and he hadn't found a single promising entry. He steeled himself to continue. Frank Rafferty and three kids, Houston town house. Mr. and Mrs. Alphonso Hodges, retirees, garage apartment in Galveston. Even through his stupefied boredom and frustration, he had to notice how good his secretary really was. Lisa must have used ten operatives to put together a list this complete.

Moses and Laterica Washington. Ahmid Bhagat and son. Cathy Kildare, Emily Rollins, Mary Sweeney—

He froze, his inner alarm sounding softly but unmistakably. Cathy Kildare, CK. It was an old saw, but a true one, that, when adopting an assumed name, people often used parts of their own names, sometimes just their initials. It felt more comfortable, perhaps, or was easier to remember, easier to match up to monogrammed luggage, shirts, handkerchiefs.

And something else tugged at his memory, too. Kildare. Something about Kildare. He struggled for the association and finally, in a flash of the good luck he'd been praying for, came up with it. Kildare, Georgia. Arthur Kearney's wife, who had died giving birth to Jennie, had been from Kildare, Georgia. Her homesickness had become legend around the Kearney house. She had once even tried to plant magnolia trees in the south forty.

Cathy Kildare. He drummed his fingers on the table. Could it be? The address was on an island called Stewart's Roost, which Michael vaguely remembered. He found it on the map, just off the coast—a tiny blob, so misshapen it looked like a water spot on the paper—and searched his memory for details. He frowned. Wasn't Stewart's Roost the most pitiful, rundown excuse for an island around these parts? He had a mental image of tacky cookie-cutter cottages and beaches so eroded they'd been almost entirely washed away in some spots.

He tried to picture the impeccable Clare Kearney living in such a place, and he couldn't. Sighing, he moved on down the list. Maria and Ted Gonzalez, John and Jean Sparkings, Liz and... But he kept going back to Cathy Kildare. His inner alarm was getting louder. It might not make any sense, but his instincts were on red alert, and he couldn't ignore them. They were going to ring bells in his head until he checked this out.

"Knock, knock?"

The coy voice came from the open doorway, and Michael whipped around, jolted out of his deep musings. It was Stephanie, and she was waving another fax at him.

"Gosh, you're a popular fellow around here, Mr. Winters," she said playfully, holding out the single sheet.

"Thanks." Taking the fax, Michael smiled, but his heart pumped a little faster. It must be something big. He knew Lisa would never pester him with anything trivial.

It was only four sentences, but he was right. The words were phrased enigmatically—Lisa was too cagey to say much that prying eyes might read—and they were far from trivial.

"Restaurants opened on overdue Mitchell money," Lisa had written. "Trust targeted. Inheritance threatened by new arrival." And then the fax ended with their code phrase for danger. "Situation unpleasant."

CHAPTER TWELVE

AUTOMATICALLY folding the fax into a small, tight square and jamming it into the pocket of his jeans, Michael strode across the room toward Jennie's office, uncomfortably aware that rest was a luxury they could no longer afford.

He had, until just this minute, remained extremely skeptical about Clare's contention that Alex was borrowing money from the Mitchells. Clare had always been the melodramatic type, and Michael knew from experience that wives could invent the most villainous depravities to lay at the door of estranged husbands.

But the phlegmatic Lisa worked only from provable facts, so Michael knew it was true. Alex Todd was in hock up to his ears to the Mitchell family. And apparently Alex had promised money from Clare's trust fund as collateral.

Michael's gut turned icy as he contemplated the layers of meaning that could be inferred from Lisa's next sentence. "Inheritance threatened by new arrival." Whose inheritance? Clare had already come into full control of the trust fund—Michael remembered that from his early investigations—so surely it was too late for a pregnancy to affect Clare's inheritance.

That left Alex, who obviously would be his wife's beneficiary. Michael hadn't looked into the terms of Clare's will—hadn't even in his most evil dreams imagined that he'd need to—but it sounded horrifyingly as if Alex stood to lose access to the money if Clare had a child before she died.

And that disturbed someone so much that Lisa would have felt the need to add those two alarming words, *situation unpleasant.*

Michael noticed a bitter, metallic taste in his mouth, and swallowing hard, he walked a little faster. Choosing to approach from the relative privacy of Jennie's side door, he moved through her secretary's office with only a cursory nod. Surprised, Stephanie stopped typing, but something in his determined stride silenced the words on her lips before she could voice them.

"Jennie?" Though his voice was unnaturally loud, there was no answer. He raised his fist to knock, but with the first touch of his knuckles the door, which should have been locked, drifted open, revealing a dark and apparently empty room. Silence flowed out in cold, oppressive waves.

"She's gone," Stephanie said unnecessarily, her tone inexplicably guilty. "She went out."

Michael didn't even look at her. Shoving the door open, he barged into the office, flicking on the light as if he couldn't believe Jennie wasn't there somewhere, hiding in the shadows. He yanked the drawstrings of the curtains. He whisked open her small closet. He even, like a damn fool, cast a quick glimpse under her desk—as if, for God's sake, Jennifer Kearney would crawl under furniture to hide like a scared rabbit. Logic didn't rule here. He just couldn't, wouldn't accept that she was gone.

But the room was uncompromisingly empty. When there was nowhere else to look, he dropped onto the sofa with an involuntary groan. Frustrated, he ran his hand over the cushions, but they retained no hint of Jennie's warmth; not a single indentation held the imprint of her body.

And, with that cool touch from which all trace of last night's passion had disappeared, it finally hit him. She really was gone. Long gone. She had dressed herself in the darkness and sneaked out the back door, all because she hadn't wanted to see him. Hadn't wanted to trust him.

He couldn't bring himself to examine the implications of that. Not now. He couldn't afford to risk emotional paralysis when, somewhere out there, Jennie might be rushing headlong into a situation more dangerous than she could imagine.

Rising in one rough movement, he grabbed the telephone, holding the receiver in fingers clenched so tight they ached, and punched in the cellular phone number of the operative he'd sent to cover Alex. He listened to the annoying electronic ring—two, three, four. Where *was* this guy? "Hello, Mencken? Winters. Got a report for me?"

"He was holed up in his hotel all of yesterday," Mencken said, his voice strangely diffident. "But then he dashed out early this morning. I've been following him east on the interstate for the past half hour. Not a whole lot of traffic this time of day, so I had to stay several car lengths behind." The man's voice took on an apologetic, defensive tone. "I had to—otherwise he would have made me. You know that's standard."

Michael's inner bell began to go off again. This sounded a lot like someone rationalizing a serious mistake. "And?"

"And I lost him."

Somehow Michael managed not to curse, although a good, gut-deep profanity might at least have siphoned off some of the incredible frustration that swamped him. "How?"

"Just rotten luck, really." Mencken's voice relaxed a little, apparently realizing that Michael wasn't going to lose his temper. "It happened about five minutes ago, right before you called. Actually I was about to call you to let you know. He'd just gone over a drawbridge, not a boat in sight, I never dreamed there would be a problem. They must have been testing the mechanism or something, though, because the barrier went down, and I was stuck behind it. By the time the bridge was back in place Todd's car was nowhere in sight.''

Damn! Michael fought the urge to criticize, though it had been stupid to keep so great a distance on the bridge. If only he was at home, he thought, where he knew which operatives were reliable enough to take on the crucial jobs. Here, working with free-lancers, he was having to make do with men he wouldn't put on the lost puppy patrol back home.

But he was wasting time. All the indignation in the world wouldn't find Alex. Michael knew he had to stay focused if there was any chance of recouping their losses. Lowering his voice, he asked Mencken to describe Alex's route in explicit detail. He shut his eyes, listening intently, searching through the words for any clue to his destination.

Gradually, a picture formed in Michael's mind. The drawbridge spanned the intracoastal, and from there several smaller bridges led to the tiny islands he had seen from Brad's backyard. One of those islands was Stewart's Roost.

His throat tightened, and his head throbbed where the telephone was pressed against his temple. God, it was such a gamble. He held so few cards—a pair of familiar initials, a drawbridge, a few grains of sand in Jennie's car. In his whole career, he'd never bet so much on so little. He dropped the phone in its cradle with hands that suddenly felt weak and damp. It wasn't enough.

But it was all he had.

As SHE LEANED out the gulfside window of the cottage, Jennie decided that, ironically, she'd never seen Stewart's Roost look better than it did now, in Clare's last hour here. A summer squall had drenched the island this morning, and every brittle palm frond had turned green and fanned gent-

ly in the balmy air. Even the underbrush looked pictur-
esque, with the sabrelike weeds suddenly sprouting pink and
yellow flowers.

The silver pillars of clouds forming on the horizon were
also charming, but Jennie knew that they meant the storm
was only taking a break. Unless they wanted to load up the
car in the rain, she and Clare needed to hustle.

"Finished in there?" she called into the kitchen, working to keep her tone upbeat. Clare had been nearly frantic
by the time Jennie arrived, having spent the two hours since
her sister was due imagining all kinds of dreadful things—
mishaps, betrayals, abductions. Jennie had decided immediately not to tell Clare anything of what had happened last
night.

"Almost," Clare called, her voice muffled. She must still
have her head in the refrigerator, trying to decide what to
bring with them and what to pitch out. Every tiny decision
was taking forever. Gone, unfortunately, was the crisp re-
alism Jennie had admired last night, and in its place was the
old Clare, the princess who sagged like a rag doll in a crisis.

But Jennie tried not to be too harsh. No one could change
completely overnight. She hoisted both of Clare's large
suitcases and hobbled into the living room.

"Just dump it all," she said breathlessly, dropping the
suitcases by the door with a thump. "You can get more
when you're settled."

"But it's such a waste," Clare said. She stared into the
refrigerator mournfully, as if it was a metaphor for her life.

"Clare," Jennie said, struggling to hold back her impa-
tience. "It's ten dollars worth of yogurt, for heaven's sake.
Dump it!" She gestured toward the front window. "Look
at the sky—it's going to rain again any minute. Let's go before—"

The words stopped as she watched her sister's face transform. Clare had obediently shifted her lethargic gaze to the window, and as soon as she did the color began to drain from her cheeks. Her eyes widened, and her lips pressed together tightly, as if they fought to hold in a cry.

Frowning, Jennie turned to see what had produced such a reaction. Surely a few thunderclouds wouldn't affect anyone so dramatically. Nothing short of a tornado spiraling right at the cottage could account for such pallor.

And then she saw. She felt her skin paling and knew that her face must be a mirror image of Clare's inarticulate horror. Just outside the window, like a convocation of silently summoned demons, three cars had materialized. They were all dark, eerily anonymous vehicles, windows tinted heavily, obscuring whoever was within. They had formed a semicircle around her little red car, mechanical vultures patiently guarding their helpless prey.

Watching them, waiting for a door to open and for someone, anyone, to emerge, Jennie felt paralyzed. Her heart was knocking so hard her ribs felt bruised, and a trickle of cold perspiration zigzagged through her hairline, but she didn't move. Behind her, Clare's breath was harsh, but she, too, seemed frozen in place.

Who? Who was it? The question echoed through Jennie's mind like a cry reverberating through a tunnel. Were the clouds pressing nearer? She had a dizzying sensation of darkness closing in around the edges of her vision, of the three cars sliding away from her, of everything getting smaller, dimmer, vaguely surreal. Had she forgotten to breathe, she wondered numbly? Her heart was hammering in her ears, as if trying frantically to tell her something . . .

She gulped air with a broken sound that shook like a gasping sob, and with a flash of painful light the world steadied a little. Probably only a couple of seconds had passed, she guessed, only a second or two that had been stretched into a lifetime by this agonizing slow-motion awareness. And then the driver of the middle car opened the door.

She knew instantly—as soon as she saw the first inch of blue jeans, the first curve of calf. The only question, really, was why she hadn't known sooner. How could she not have recognized the uniquely reptilian slant of those headlights, the snakelike undulation of the lines on that car? It was Michael's Jaguar, and as time resumed its normal speed, the man who climbed briskly out of the low-slung seat was Michael himself, grim-faced and intent.

"Oh, God, I told you so!" Clare's intense voice was full of terror and fury. Then she moaned, a low, heartsick sound. "I knew you'd tell him. I knew it."

Jennie didn't answer her—there was no time for excuses or denials. Perversely, the slow motion of shock had given over to the fast forward of fear, and suddenly the other car doors were opening, too, and men spilled out, calling to one another, slamming doors and crunching across the shell-lined drive.

The first car belonged to Alex, who was sitting in the first seat. When he saw Michael he whisked out, tension evident in each coiled muscle of his body, and stormed toward the cottage. Michael followed, and as the two men met in the driveway, Michael put his hand on Alex's arm, holding him back for a quick, heated conference. The last person to emerge was a stranger, a thin man with round glasses who seemed less intense, less involved than the others.

At the sight of him, Jennie's breath came out in a long, heartfelt release. She didn't know what his part was in all this, but she realized she had been expecting the ugly, lined face of a Mitchell. Any other face could only bring relief.

"Quick!" Clare's voice had the unmistakable note of panic. "We've got to get out of here!"

Jennie's mind raced wildly, tearing through the maze of emotions, trying to formulate a plan. But she simply ran in mental circles, unable to catch any idea that was even remotely workable. She should have thought this through long ago, she berated herself. She should have had a bodyguard, a gun, an escape route... But those words were from a foreign language she had never learned to speak. And, in spite of everything, she'd never really believed it would come to this. Never.

She looked again. Alex and Michael, finished with their conversation, were almost at the front door.

"Out the back," Jennie said impulsively, pointing to the kitchen door, which opened onto the beach. Clare looked confused but trusting, and she turned immediately to obey the curt order.

The responsibility implicit in such absolute faith was unnerving, and Jennie wished she could feel worthy of that trust. She tried to look confident. "There's a little beachfront bar about five or six lots south of here. Do you remember it?"

Clare frowned, concentrating, then relaxed. "Oh, yes," she said. "I know it."

"Good. Head there." Jennie herded Clare toward the door. "At least there will be other people around. We'll be out in the open, and we won't be alone."

Then the noise she'd been dreading finally came. More a pounding than a knock—the demand of a man who resents the fact that the door is closed to him at all. The knock of a man who will, if necessary, feel justified in battering the door right off the hinges.

Fear—real surging, burning fear, not that insipid anxiety she had once labeled with the word—exploded inside her, as if it had been a bomb planted in her chest waiting for the moment when it would be detonated by the sound of that pounding.

"Run!" She threw open the kitchen door, practically shoving Clare out into the overcast morning. Clare lunged forward, her tennis shoes silent on the path that led through the underbrush to the beach. Jennie tried to follow, got as far as the sand, but her less-sensible sandals dug into the loosely shifting surface, slowing her like a clutch of hands in a nightmare, and she fell, twisting her ankle viciously.

She wanted to cry, but it was impossible to cry when she couldn't breathe, when her lungs had turned to stone in her chest. Scrambling upright, she ignored the stabbing pain and slogged through the sand, painfully putting a few meager yards between herself and the cottage. Clare hadn't gotten much farther—she was only ten yards or so ahead.

Surely by now the men were beyond the feigned civility of knocking. Perhaps they were pushing against the flimsy door, or perhaps they had guessed that the women were no longer cowering behind the curtains, waiting submissively to be caught. Michael would figure it out first, she thought. She could imagine him sprinting to the back of the cottage, seeing the gaping door still swaying from their turbulent exit, looking furiously up the beach, then down, spotting them . . .

Suddenly something grabbed her shoulder. Not something—someone. With a terrified gasp she stumbled and then swayed on her heels, into Michael's waiting arms.

He kept her from falling, and with rough fingers he turned her around to face him. His rugged features were stormy, brows drawn down hard over dark eyes.

"Damn it, Jennie," he said, his words as low and harsh as the thunder that boomed in the distance. "What the hell—"

"Oh, Jennie, no!" Clare's terrified wail came from only a dozen yards down the beach, not far enough for safety, Jennie thought with a sinking heart. She whipped her head around and saw Clare standing still, obviously paralyzed with fearful indecision. Clare looked longingly down the beach toward the bar and then looked at Jennie, as if she struggled with her conscience. Run for safety or stay to help her sister? The question contorted her pretty face. "Jennie?"

"Run." Jennie somehow forced the word out, hoping it was loud enough for Clare to hear. "Run!"

Clare didn't need to be asked again. She swiveled and resumed running, angling down the beach toward the shoreline, where the wet sand provided better purchase for her churning legs. *"Run?"* The word exploded from Michael's lips, and it seemed to hang on the wet, dense air, floating like a half-visible barrier between them. "Are you running from *me,* Jennie?"

She wanted to answer, wanted to fling a cruel yes into that angry face that had betrayed her so heartlessly. But her gaze was caught by a motion just behind his shoulder, and the word couldn't get past the thick lump of fear that suddenly rose in her throat.

Alex and the third man had jogged around the side of the cottage. Alex's face was twisted and pale with emotion, and he was yelling something, some hoarse, distorted syllables that the wind blew away before she could quite make them out.

But she could tell by his rough hand gestures that he was commanding her to wait. He had already begun loping across the walkway, his legs diabolically efficient on the sand that had proved so dangerous to her. And in that moment, as he closed the distance between them, she hated him, hated the weakness in his chin, the vanity in his neat little mustache, the self-indulgence in the expensive cut of his linen trousers.

Oh, God, she should have called the police days ago. Why had she listened to Clare, who obviously clung to an irrational hope that some new revelation would miraculously exonerate her husband? Jennie, eager to keep Clare calm, had been too compliant. Now there was no time to get away.

No time at all. Thanks to Michael. Her lover. She turned her defeated face to him.

"How could you, Michael?" Tears blurred her voice and her vision. "How could you bring him here?"

"*Bring* him?" His flush deepened, but somehow Jennie knew it wasn't shame that colored his cheekbones. It was more like the dull glow of molten steel. She could almost see liquid metal flow through him, replacing flesh and bone with a rapidly hardening, impenetrable shield. His chin rose, and his back slowly stiffened.

And then, suddenly, Alex was upon them.

"Where is she, Jennie?" Alex was standing too close. Jennie could hear the labored rasp of his breathing as he cast his eyes frantically up and down the beach. "Where did she go?" He wiped sweat from his forehead, and then from his mustache. "I have to talk to her. You don't know how important it is!"

Jennie couldn't answer him. She averted her eyes, unable even to look at him now that he was so monstrously transformed by her suspicions and his sweating agitation.

"Damn!" Alex turned to Michael. "Did you see her go?"

Michael didn't answer immediately, and the silence was painful. Jennie found herself holding her breath. She knew he'd watched Clare—it would be so easy for him to point Alex in the right direction. *Don't tell him, don't tell him,* her inner voice begged, and she closed her eyes, willing him to hear.

But, her more practical side argued, did it really matter anyway? The bar had never been an escape—it had merely been a blind, subconscious instinct that they'd be safer in a public place than in the isolation of the little cottage.

"Maybe," Michael said quietly. "But I need to know what you want with her first."

"She's my wife," Alex returned bitterly, biting the words out. His hands were clenched in white-knuckled fists. "I have the right to talk to her."

"About what?" Still quiet, but implacable.

Alex seemed enraged by Michael's air of immovable authority. "Listen, Winters—" He thrust aggressively forward, apparently too wrought up to remember that he was at least four inches shorter than Michael and physically no match for him. "This doesn't concern you."

To Jennie's surprise, the third man, who'd been watching passively, stepped up behind Alex and cleared his throat pointedly. "Could you use a hand, Mr. Winters?"

Without taking his gaze from Alex, Michael shook his head. "Not yet," he said mildly, and like a trained pet, the man in the glasses stepped back.

Jennie was mystified. Who was he? Someone who worked for Michael, undoubtedly, but why had Michael brought him along? She didn't have time to sort it out, because Alex's temper had reached full boil. Completely out of control, he advanced threateningly toward Michael, shoving him with both palms.

"Your goon here doesn't scare me, Michael. I've dealt with people who could have this guy for breakfast!"

"Like the Mitchells?" Michael hadn't moved. He didn't sway even an inch under Alex's jabbing hands, but Jennie could tell that his temper was building. He wouldn't take much more. She wondered why Alex couldn't see it, too.

"Yeah, like the Mitchells," Alex admitted, his voice wild. "Does that shock you, Michael? You always thought you were better than Quinn and me, didn't you? Too good to need people like the Mitchells. Hell no, not you. You were a real saint. Except, of course, with Brooke."

A pulse twitched dangerously in Michael's temple, and Jennie wanted to cry out, to warn Alex to shut up. But he didn't. He didn't have the sense to see the danger. A crowd was milling around now, attracted, no doubt, by all the shouting.

Alex's shoving became more violent as his verbal abuse escalated. "Well, you never did know what you were talking about, you sanctimonious son of a—"

He never completed the insult. Finally pushed beyond his endurance, Michael responded with a swift, flashing uppercut that caught Alex squarely on the jaw. Jennie heard the sickening sound of bone against bone as, with a defeated moan, Alex went down like a bowling pin, clutching his face with both hands.

"Oh, God," Alex groaned over and over again, as if the blow had knocked all the furious verbiage right out of him. He rocked on his knees in the sand. "Oh, God, what am I going to do? They're after Clare." He sobbed, tears and dirt running between his fingers. "What'll I do?"

"*Alex!* Oh, no. No!"

Jennie looked up, astonished to hear Clare's voice. She must have been watching the encounter from the safety of the crowd, because suddenly she came flying to her husband's side.

"Alex, are you all right?" Murmuring soft, distressed noises, she knelt beside him, one arm around his shoulders, and tried to lift his head. "Are you okay?"

With a muffled cry of mingled incredulity and relief, Alex threw his arms around his wife, running his sandy hands through her hair. "Clare!" he said, burrowing his contorted face in her shoulder. "Oh, God, Clare!"

Jennie stared numbly at the pair kneeling on the sand, hardly able to believe her eyes. Oblivious to everyone else, they clung to each other as if they would, without the other to hang onto, be swept away.

Too exhausted to fully understand, she shivered at the sight and noticed for the first time that the air had grown colder. The storm. Amazingly, she had forgotten all about it. As fat drops of cold rain dashed against her hair, she raised her gaze to the sky. The clouds pressed dark and low.

Clare and Alex didn't seem to notice the rain, though even the most curious onlookers had begun to scatter for cover. With raindrops streaming down her cheeks, Jennie turned toward Michael, a bewildered question in her eyes. He was already staring at her, his face gray in the silver light.

"I think we should go in," he said flatly. "It's time we all got some answers."

CHAPTER THIRTEEN

THEY WERE a bedraggled group as they moved around the cramped living room. Jennie judged what her own condition must be from looking at Clare—wet and sandy, her fine, blond hair hanging limply around her pale face, her soggy clothes clinging to her body. Sheets of rain coated the windows, washing everyone an underwater gray. They looked as if they truly belonged in this pitiful little house, Jennie thought.

All except for Michael. Perversely, as if to torment her, the rain just made his thick, dark hair look richer and glossier, and his damp shirt merely outlined the masculinity of his broad shoulders. It would take more than a little rain to reduce him to drowned-rat status.

Of them all, Alex looked the most miserable. In spite of Clare's tender attention, his jaw had turned a muddy purple under its dusting of sand. He sat on the sofa, his head in his hands, as if he couldn't bring himself to face any of them, including his wife.

"Let's get on with it, Alex," Michael said, finally breaking the gloomy silence that had fallen over the room. He was leaning against the Formica island that separated the kitchen from the living room. "Let's don't waste time. If you could find Clare, and I could find her, anyone can find her."

Clare glanced up, her hand stilling as she smoothed Alex's hair from his sandy forehead. Obviously Michael's words unsettled her, but she didn't speak. She regarded Michael for a moment with somber eyes, then resumed her gentle stroking.

"I know. I know." Alex drew in a shaky breath. "It's simple, really. I owe the Mitchells money. A lot. I've owed them money since I was in college," he added, staring at his hands, which dangled between his knees. "My father wasn't very sympathetic about... things, so I borrowed what I needed." He shook his head slowly. "It wasn't much, really, back then. Not compared to what it is now."

Clare's breath caught raggedly, but still no one spoke. Michael was as motionless as a statue, watching Alex through hooded eyes. The thin man, who had introduced himself to Jennie as Bruce Mencken, a free-lance detective, was waiting on the front porch. And Jennie didn't dare speak, though questions swirled in her mind like smoke. She felt she had stepped into a nightmare world where she didn't know the rules and might easily make a dangerous mistake.

"Anyway," Alex continued when it became clear no one was going to prompt him, "after Quinn died, I was planning to use the insurance money to pay them off, even though I wanted to open the restaurants, but they suggested that I just go ahead and get the restaurants started, and then, when I was making money, I could pay them back and I'd never even really notice it. They even loaned me more, to help me get going."

The rambling, defensive sentences dwindled to a halt, and as if suddenly finding himself out of ammunition, he raised his head. His red-rimmed eyes were shocking in his pale face.

He looked at Clare. "But I didn't make any money, or not enough, anyway. The interest kept piling up, and they started in on me. They were getting ugly, Clare. I had to tell them something to buy some time." He swallowed, his forehead creasing with the effort. "So I told them about the trust fund."

For the first time since Alex had begun speaking, Clare's wide blue eyes flickered with doubt. Her gaze faltered, then lowered, and she stared at her lap. As if panicked by the withdrawal of her silent support, Alex grabbed her passive hands and squeezed them between his own.

"I swear, Clare, I really thought I'd be able to pay it back before your thirtieth birthday, really I did. I opened that new franchise, you know, the one in Jersey? I thought that would help." He shook her hands lightly, as if trying to get through to her, but she refused to look up. "It should have helped."

"Obviously, though, it didn't." Michael had shifted impatiently, crossing his arms over his chest. "I think we could have filled in this part of the story on our own, Alex. Why don't you just cut to the chase?"

Flushing, Alex tossed an offended scowl toward the other man, as if he had forgotten that the room held anyone but his wife. "The chase?" he echoed angrily.

"Right." Michael didn't seem fazed by the tone or the look. "You know—the important things. We have to assume, since you're here alone, that you haven't yet told them where Clare is. But have they started looking for her? Do they know she's pregnant? And is it possible that the pregnancy could be a problem because her will cuts you out in favor of any children?"

Michael's voice, as he ticked off these atrocities, was dangerously calm, but his gleaming brown eyes were as hard as stone. Jennie wondered what appalling situations he must confront regularly that he could accept this one so easily. Her mind kept balking, as if it had been pushed to the cliff edge of acceptable reality and asked to jump.

"So let's get serious, Todd," Michael finished flatly. "The bottom line here is, how can Clare protect herself?"

Clare made a small, whimpering sound of distress, and Alex whirled to face her. "Sweetheart, don't," he said frantically, pulling her hands to his chest. "It's going to be okay, really. That's why I was trying to find you. You see—" he swallowed again "—I want you to divorce me."

Clare's whimper swelled to a sob, but Alex hushed her. "It's the only way—I've thought it all through. I've already had the papers drawn up. All you have to do is sign them."

Clare looked undone, and Jennie felt her throat closing. It might not be the wisest plan—already she could see a dozen flaws, the most critical being that it would take weeks for a divorce to go through—but it did seem to be a heartfelt attempt to protect Clare. Jennie cast a quick glance at Michael, to see if he was similarly moved, but his face was unreadable.

She looked at her sister. Two tears coursed slowly down Clare's pale cheeks as she raised her face to Alex.

"I don't know whether I want a divorce," she said, her voice surprisingly steady. "But I do know that I want to pay those bastards every cent you owe them. I want them out of our lives."

Alex's jaw dropped open slightly. "No," he said in a stunned voice. "No, Clare—"

"Yes," she insisted firmly, though the tears continued to flow. "I don't want my child's father shot down in the streets, or whatever it is those people do." She reclaimed her hands, and then she wiped both cheeks, as if symbolically pulling herself together. "There's just one thing I have to ask you, Alex. There's just one thing I have to know first."

Jennie's heart started to beat double time. She knew what Clare was going to ask, and she felt as anxious about the answer as if her own future hung in the balance. She flicked another glance at Michael, to see if he knew what was coming. His ramrod-straight, iron-tense posture was her answer. He had the air of a convicted man awaiting a judge's sentence.

Alex, however, apparently had no such divination. He looked completely mystified. "What?"

"I want to know," Clare said, speaking very slowly as if this was a difficult passage she had rehearsed, "if your debts to the Mitchell family had anything to do with Quinn's death."

To Jennie's horror, Alex did not look shocked. He looked . . . She supposed the word was uncomfortable.

"Not *my* debts," he said. "But maybe his."

Clare's brows drew together sharply. "His?" She shook her head, rejecting the notion even before she fully understood it. "What are you talking about? What do you mean *his?*"

"I mean Quinn was settling his own debts that night," Alex answered. "He owed the Mitchells money, too, and they offered us both the same deal. If we'd look the other way during the robbery, they'd forget about the debt. I turned it down, but he went for it. You see, he owed them a lot more than I did."

Clare's wide eyes were blank with shock, and Jennie wondered if her own gaze was similarly unfocused. She felt that reeling, telescoping sensation she recognized as the prelude to a faint, and she took a long, deliberate breath. Oh, God . . .

Alex shot a glance toward Michael, who still, Jennie saw, hadn't moved a muscle. He was staring at Alex with a disturbing intensity. Jennie clamped down on a shiver of foreboding.

"The only thing Quinn had to do, really," Alex said, still facing Michael, "was see that Michael wasn't at the warehouse that night. But, with Brooke's help, that wasn't very difficult. She definitely knew how to keep Michael occupied."

With a painful empathy, Jennie knew that Alex's words would slice through Michael like daggers. And she was right. As Alex finished, Michael squeezed his eyes shut violently, and he tilted his head back in one fierce spasm of pain against the cabinet.

It was too much. Jennie's numb tension broke like a dam, and she burst into an uncontrollable flood of accusations.

"For God's sake, Alex, how could you? Why didn't you ever tell anyone?" She flashed to her feet, on fire with outrage, her knees shaking. "Why didn't you tell the police? You could have seen to it that the Mitchells rotted in jail. And look what you've done to the rest of us, to *Michael!* Why did you—?"

She was surprised to hear the waver of tears in her voice. She didn't feel like crying—she felt like screaming, raging, pounding. "Oh, God, Alex, why?" Maddeningly, it was tears that won the battle for her emotions. "Why did you let us blame Michael all these years?"

"The Mitchells insisted they didn't do it," Alex blurted out miserably, ignoring her last question. "I don't know—maybe something went wrong, something got out of hand and Quinn got killed accidently. I swear, I never really knew what happened." He rubbed his forehead. "You don't know what these people are like! They said I couldn't ever tell anyone about their original offer, because then I'd be implicated, too, even if anyone could ever prove it, which they couldn't. Besides, you know the police already suspected them, and they couldn't prove a thing. So maybe they didn't... Maybe it was just a coincidence...."

But he obviously heard how weak that sounded, and he let the stream of gushing self-defense trickle out into a muddy slog of stagnant half sentences. Jennie stared at him mercilessly, knowing that her disgust and disbelief were written all over her face. She didn't give a damn about how vulnerable he had been. As far as she was concerned, they should have locked him up in the same cell with those monsters and thrown away the key.

Sensing no quarter from Jennie, Alex turned to Clare with an air of helpless entreaty. "And I was in love with you, Clare. I wanted to marry you. I knew you'd never forgive me if you'd thought I had any part in Quinn's death. But Michael— Well, he wasn't even one of us, really, and it didn't seem to matter so much what you thought of him—"

At that, Michael's control finally broke. With a deep, vicious growl that was beyond words, he turned toward Alex. For a terrifying moment Jennie thought he might kill him, simply take his neck between his hands and strangle him.

But somehow Michael stopped himself. Halfway across the room he froze.

"No," he said between clenched teeth, the words coming out like bullets. "You're not worth going to jail for. I think I'll just let the Mitchells take care of you. It's their kind of work, disposing of garbage."

Then he turned and, shoving open the kitchen door, walked out onto the small back porch, in spite of the rain that poured from the eaves, as if he was desperate for clean air to breathe.

Jennie watched him go, her heart pounding, longing to run after him. But she just stood there, in a limbo in the middle of the room, halfway between the sister she had vowed to protect and the man she had tried not to love.

A small cough attracted her fragmented attention. Mencken had quietly opened the front door. He smiled sheepishly.

"Go ahead," he said, his voice surprisingly kind. "I can baby-sit in here if you'd like." He inclined his head toward the pair on the sofa. "Though I don't really think he's going to be any more trouble."

Slow to process the implications, Jennie turned her head toward her sister. Clare and Alex sat hand in hand, and in spite of every dreadful thing that had been said in this room, Clare gazed at her husband with the love-tortured expression she'd worn since Michael had knocked him to the ground.

A month ago, even a week ago, Jennie would have been incredulous, scornfully judgmental. But today, God help her, she understood. Clare loved Alex, and by some mysterious alchemy, she didn't see him the same way Jennie did. Jennie saw base selfishness, criminal weakness, despicable snobbishness, and was disgusted. Clare saw only the man she loved.

And, after all, who was Jennie to judge? Last night, though her mind been filled with terrifying doubts, her heart had cried for Michael, her body had ached for him. It had made no difference to her whether Michael was villain or hero, whether her decision to love was wisdom or folly.

And perhaps, she thought as she watched Alex kiss Clare's hand, that was as it should be. Perhaps everyone needed someone who was blind to their faults, who forgave and healed and sustained whether it was deserved or not. Maybe, because of that, love could be the flower that bloomed on barren ground, the melody that soared above the grim cacophony of life.

Out there on the porch stood the one man who could be all that for her. Was it possible, she wondered, for love to work its magic again? Could anything transform her in his eyes from the angry, faithless accuser who had hurt him time and time again? She felt the lowering swoop of hopelessness, remembering the things she'd said. Forgiveness seemed, suddenly, too much to expect.

But she had to try. She at least had to tell him she was sorry, so profoundly sorry...

"I think I will go out for a bit," she said, managing a watery smile for Mencken. "Thanks," she added, hoping he could sense her gratitude, though she couldn't find the words. She didn't bother to speak to Clare and Alex—they would be as unaware of her absence as they were of her presence.

She opened the kitchen door quietly and stepped outside. Perhaps the drumming of the rain on the roof drowned any noise she made, but if Michael heard her he gave no sign. Taking a deep breath, she stepped to the edge of the porch, so close to him he couldn't have failed to notice, but still he didn't speak.

The storm was equally unwelcoming. Rain dashed against the wooden railing, spraying a fine, cool mist onto her face, as if it tried to push her back into the house. It stung her lips, filled her lashes like tears. She could hear the restless roar of the gulf, could see it just beyond the rain. It looked angry, tossing foam-tipped waves toward the cottage.

But she held her ground. She gripped the sodden rail, ignoring the rivulets of rain that ran between her fingers.

"I'm sorry," she said, because it was the only thing she could think to say, but still he didn't move, merely stared out into the distance as if he hadn't heard. She wondered what he saw there. Ghosts, perhaps? Were there sad, silver ghosts moving somewhere in that endless gray downpour? Quinn, Brooke, the son he'd never have...

"I'm so sorry," she said again, whispering this time, her voice blending with the sibilant rush of waves against the sand. "We were wrong, horribly wrong to think you were involved in Quinn's death or that you would have led harm to Clare today."

He shifted sharply, and the motion took him another inch away from her physically—a million miles away emotionally. "Don't worry about it, Jennie," he said dully. "It doesn't matter anymore."

"It does to me." She wondered, though, whether it mattered to *him* anymore. Alex's confession might have finally set Michael free. Perhaps guilt had been the only cord that tethered him to their lives. And now the cord had been broken.

"I don't expect you to forgive us," she hurried on, terrified by the thought of him leaving them behind for good. "We don't deserve it." She blinked away a blur of rain tears. "Especially me."

Finally he looked at her, though his set, grim face was not a sight to raise her hopes. "Why especially you?"

She forced herself to loosen her grip on the railing. Her whole face was damp. "I should have believed in you," she said, pushing back a strand of hair and wiping her cheeks impotently with a hand that was equally wet. But at least the gesture hid her miserable flush from his intense scrutiny. "I should have trusted you because...because I was the one who loved you."

He laughed, a short, ugly sound, and turned away. "Oh, *that.*"

"Yes," she cried, acutely pained by his dismissal of the word and all the word implied. "That." She grabbed his arm. "Why do you laugh? Don't you believe it? Don't you remember I told you so last night?"

He whipped his face around. Sharp raindrops were flung from his hair, imbedding in her skin like tiny needles. "Yes, you did, didn't you?" He stared at her hand, pale against his arm. "And then this morning you ran from me as if the demons of hell were after you." He raised his gaze, and it was full of furious betrayal. "Are you trying to tell me that you could love me and think me a demon at the same moment?"

She stared into those angry eyes, afraid that she might lose her nerve. Would he, who had known so much abuse in his life, care what self-serving explanations she could invent for hers?

"Yes," she said as bravely as she could, though her throat was a tight column of pain. "That's exactly what I'm telling you. I've loved you since I was so young I didn't know what the word meant. I loved you when you were my brother's friend, and I loved you when I thought you had let him die."

He narrowed his eyes, and she inhaled the dense, moist air, trying to brace herself. "I loved you last night, when you were in my arms." She bit her lip, hoping the pain would drive away the foolish tears that threatened to spill over her wet cheeks. "And I'll love you still, when you leave me."

A hoarse, rough sound escaped him, a sound that carried the sweeping force of the tide as it ground mercilessly against the sand. The muscles of his arm bunched beneath her palm.

"Jennie, I—"

"And you are going to leave me," she said, lifting her gaze to his. "Aren't you?" She began to cry helplessly, though she knew he would hate it. "You're going back to Seattle, and you're going to try to forget that you ever knew us."

"I should," he said fiercely. He put his hand over hers and pressed it into his arm so tightly she could feel the blood pulsing in his veins. "I should! I don't feel anything there, nothing at all. I'm safe there, Jennie. Not a soul in Seattle can hurt me the way you can."

"Oh, Michael—" She was mute with shame. He was right, so absolutely right in wanting to leave. How could she ask him to stay when her family had brought him only pain? But how could she let him go? She loved him so much, loved every inch of his beautiful body, every lonely acre of his courageous spirit.

"I love you," she said again, though she knew it had the same manipulative, begging quality that Alex's protestations had possessed. She couldn't help it. She couldn't live without him. If only he would allow it, she would spend the rest of her life trying to make up for the pain they had caused him. She put her other hand on him, on the muscles of his chest, which were clearly defined by the sodden fabric of his shirt. She placed her fingers just under his heart, capturing its deep rhythm like the sensual beat of dark, unseen wings against her palm. "Please," she whispered. "Please don't leave me."

"I should," he repeated, his voice thick. And then, ducking his head, he groaned. "But, God help me, I can't."

The throbbing quickened under her hand, as if the madly beating wings were struggling to soar. "I learned to live again last night," he said, "and, however much it hurts, I just can't go back to being safe and dead again."

"Last night?" She knew what he meant, but she wanted him to say it. She wanted him to say that it was making love to her that had brought him back to life. She wanted to be sure.

"Yes. Last night." Turning to her, he gathered her slowly in his arms. She went with a piercing pleasure, knowing she would fit perfectly against his chest, knowing she could never feel fully complete unless she was touching him. "Last night—when you loved me."

Just as they had once before, their bodies merged easily, from shoulder to knee, like two raindrops twinning to follow the same softly curving path. For a moment it was enough just to be touching. And then, so slowly, he lifted her face to his, his gaze sweeping over every feature as if to memorize her. His eyes were as dark as night, and a frantic pulse beat in his temple. Then finally, with a groan of hunger, he lowered his head to hers.

Was it possible for a mere kiss to reach all the way into her, to transfer heat from one tortured nerve ending to another, until all of her body was melting? No, not possible, but happening nonetheless. Her legs were weak. She clasped her hands around his neck for stability, but ended up pulling him to her greedily, wanting even more—more melting, more weakness, more of everything that was Michael.

She parted her lips, and he dove in with a hot, dark thrust, then again and again, until the rhythm drove her mad, drove her hips up against his, seeking the mate to that rhythm. He wrapped his hands around her bottom, kneading and stroking. As the wet folds of his stiff jeans grazed against her legs, she remembered with a shiver of wanton desire that she wore no underclothes.

With regret he pulled his mouth from hers. "You are dangerous, Jennie," he said with a shaky attempt at levity. He dropped a final kiss on her neck and caressed the curve of her hip one last time before taking his hands away. "I haven't a shred of self-control when I'm with you."

"Good," she said, and her voice was trembling, too. "I don't want you to." But three people waited inside—and so many painful decisions still remained for them all. She knew that they couldn't give in to this passion now.

Sighing, she rested her cheek against his heart. She brought one hand up to trace the muscles of his chest, to toy with the male nipple that pebbled under his damp shirt. "You were alive last night—you could feel last night. What about today?"

"I'm still alive," he said, a genuinely playful tone creeping into his throaty voice for the first time. "Or hadn't you noticed?" He stroked her hair gently. "I have a feeling I'll always be alive when I'm with you."

"Oh, yes." She smiled into his shirt. "So you must come live with me," she said dreamily, "and be my love."

"That sounds suspiciously like a Brad McIntosh poetry special."

She laughed softly, delighted to hear the jealous note in his voice. He did care. Though his life had been too difficult to allow him to express love easily, he clearly did care. She would make do with that. With that—and with the promise of his arms to hold her night after endless, melting night.

"It is. And Brad taught me another quote, too," she said, looking at him with tears shimmering in her eyes. The clouds had begun to part. Patches of golden sunshine flashed like jewels set in the silver curtain of rain. "Want to hear it?"

He nodded warily. "I suppose so."

"So dear I love him," she began, hoping her voice would hold out, "that with him all deaths I could endure, without him live no life."

For a long moment Michael didn't say anything. But she thought she saw a rainbow drop glimmer on his lashes, and when he finally spoke his voice was husky.

"Yes," he said. "Very eloquent. But you listen to me, sweet Jennie. I think you're going to have to tell the good professor that it would be unseemly for a married lady to take poetry lessons.''

Married . . . Her heart lifted on a sudden gust of joy. She smiled into his eyes, her tears finally disappearing. "Except from her husband," she teased, folding her body against his with a new and wonderful heat. Her husband . . .

"Yes," he echoed with a catch in his throat. "Except from me."

And then, lowering his head to hers once more, he took her face in his hands. "I love you, Jennie," he said, his breath warm against her skin. "There aren't enough words in all of Shakespeare for me to tell you how much."

"Then don't use words," she said, her joy so intense she didn't think she could bear it. "Love me in silence."

As she spoke, a hot, golden flame leaped behind his eyes, but he gathered her into his arms without a word, and he kissed her slowly, deeply, silently. With a poetry more beautiful than any she'd ever known, his heart sang to hers in that sweet, scented silence, and their pure, unbroken melody floated high above the storm.

1994 MISTLETOE MARRIAGES
HISTORICAL CHRISTMAS STORIES

With a twinkle of lights and a flurry of snowflakes, Harlequin Historicals presents *Mistletoe Marriages*, a collection of four of the most magical stories by your favorite historical authors. The perfect way to celebrate the season!

Brimming with romance and good cheer, these heartwarming stories will be available in November wherever Harlequin books are sold.

RENDEZVOUS by Elaine Barbieri
THE WOLF AND THE LAMB by Kathleen Eagle
CHRISTMAS IN THE VALLEY by Margaret Moore
KEEPING CHRISTMAS by Patricia Gardner Evans

Add a touch of romance to your holiday with
Mistletoe Marriages Christmas Stories!

HARLEQUIN®

MMXS94

Where do you find hot Texas nights, smooth Texas charm and dangerously sexy cowboys?

Crystal Creek reverberates with the exciting rhythm of Texas. Each story features the rugged individuals who live and love in the Lone Star state.

"...Crystal Creek wonderfully evokes the hot days and steamy nights of a small Texas community...impossible to put down until the last page is turned."
—*Romantic Times*

"...a series that should hook any romance reader. Outstanding."
—*Rendezvous*

"Altogether, it couldn't be better." —*Rendezvous*

Don't miss the next book in this exciting series. Look for
SOMEWHERE OTHER THAN THE NIGHT by SANDY STEEN

Available in December wherever Harlequin books are sold.

IT'S FREE! IT'S FUN! ENTER THE

☆ **"Hooray for** ☆
☆ **Hollywood"** ☆

SWEEPSTAKES!

We're giving away prizes to celebrate the screening of four new romance movies on CBS TV this fall! Look for the movies on four Sunday afternoons in October. And be sure to return your Official Entry Coupons to try for a fabulous vacation in Hollywood!

☆ If you're the Grand Prize winner we'll fly you and your companion to Los Angeles for a 7-day/6-night vacation you'll never forget!

☆ You'll stay at the luxurious Regent Beverly Wilshire Hotel,* a prime location for celebrity spotting!

☆ You'll have time to visit Universal Studios,* stroll the Hollywood Walk of Fame, check out celebrities' footprints at Mann's Chinese Theater, ride a trolley to see the homes of the stars, and more!

☆ The prize includes a rental car for 7 days and $1,000.00 pocket money!

Someone's going to win this fabulous prize, and it might just be you! Remember, the more times you enter, the better your chances of winning!

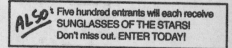

ALSO Five hundred entrants will each receive SUNGLASSES OF THE STARS! Don't miss out. ENTER TODAY!

"HOORAY FOR HOLLYWOOD" SWEEPSTAKES

HERE'S HOW THE SWEEPSTAKES WORKS

OFFICIAL RULES — NO PURCHASE NECESSARY

To enter, complete an Official Entry Form or hand print on a 3" x 5" card the words "HOORAY FOR HOLLYWOOD", your name and address and mail your entry in the pre-addressed envelope (if provided) or to: "Hooray for Hollywood" Sweepstakes, P.O. Box 9076, Buffalo, NY 14269-9076 or "Hooray for Hollywood" Sweepstakes, P.O. Box 637, Fort Erie, Ontario L2A 5X3. Entries must be sent via First Class Mail and be received no later than 12/31/94. No liability is assumed for lost, late or misdirected mail.

Winners will be selected in random drawings to be conducted no later than January 31, 1995 from all eligible entries received.

Grand Prize: A 7-day/6-night trip for 2 to Los Angeles, CA including round trip air transportation from commercial airport nearest winner's residence, accommodations at the Regent Beverly Wilshire Hotel, free rental car, and $1,000 spending money. (Approximate prize value which will vary dependent upon winner's residence: $5,400.00 U.S.); 500 Second Prizes: A pair of "Hollywood Star" sunglasses (prize value: $9.95 U.S. each). Winner selection is under the supervision of D.L. Blair, Inc., an independent judging organization, whose decisions are final. Grand Prize travelers must sign and return a release of liability prior to traveling. Trip must be taken by 2/1/96 and is subject to airline schedules and accommodations availability.

Sweepstakes offer is open to residents of the U.S. (except Puerto Rico) and Canada who are 18 years of age or older, except employees and immediate family members of Harlequin Enterprises, Ltd., its affiliates, subsidiaries, and all agencies, entities or persons connected with the use, marketing or conduct of this sweepstakes. All federal, state, provincial, municipal and local laws apply. Offer void wherever prohibited by law. Taxes and/or duties are the sole responsibility of the winners. Any litigation within the province of Quebec respecting the conduct and awarding of prizes may be submitted to the Regie des loteries et courses du Quebec. All prizes will be awarded; winners will be notified by mail. No substitution of prizes are permitted. Odds of winning are dependent upon the number of eligible entries received.

Potential grand prize winner must sign and return an Affidavit of Eligibility within 30 days of notification. In the event of non-compliance within this time period, prize may be awarded to an alternate winner. Prize notification returned as undeliverable may result in the awarding of prize to an alternate winner. By acceptance of their prize, winners consent to use of their names, photographs, or likenesses for purpose of advertising, trade and promotion on behalf of Harlequin Enterprises, Ltd., without further compensation unless prohibited by law. A Canadian winner must correctly answer an arithmetical skill-testing question in order to be awarded the prize.

For a list of winners (available after 2/28/95), send a separate stamped, self-addressed envelope to: Hooray for Hollywood Sweepstakes 3252 Winners, P.O. Box 4200, Blair, NE 68009.

OFFICIAL ENTRY COUPON

"Hooray for Hollywood"
SWEEPSTAKES!

Yes, I'd love to win the Grand Prize — a vacation in Hollywood — or one of 500 pairs of "sunglasses of the stars"! Please enter me in the sweepstakes!

This entry must be received by December 31, 1994.
Winners will be notified by January 31, 1995.

Name _____

Address _____ Apt. _____

City _____

State/Prov. _____ Zip/Postal Code _____

Daytime phone number _____
(area code)

Account # _____

Return entries with invoice in envelope provided. Each book in this shipment has two entry coupons — and the more coupons you enter, the better your chances of winning!

DIRCBS

OFFICIAL ENTRY COUPON

"Hooray for Hollywood"
SWEEPSTAKES!

Yes, I'd love to win the Grand Prize — a vacation in Hollywood — or one of 500 pairs of "sunglasses of the stars"! Please enter me in the sweepstakes!

This entry must be received by December 31, 1994.
Winners will be notified by January 31, 1995.

Name _____

Address _____ Apt. _____

City _____

State/Prov. _____ Zip/Postal Code _____

Daytime phone number _____
(area code)

Account # _____

Return entries with invoice in envelope provided. Each book in this shipment has two entry coupons — and the more coupons you enter, the better your chances of winning!

DIRCBS